ACCLAIM FOR BY LIGHT AND LOVE

"The romance is complex but also complete, full of grace and selfless love."

—ERIN PHILLIPS, number one bestselling author of *A Crown of Chains*

"With vivid imagery and depth of heart, Anna Augustine weaves together a short and sweet love story. Her characters and world feel so real that they could leap off the page."

—ALISSA J. ZAVALIANOS, Author of *The Earth-Treader* and *Endlewood*

"*By Light and Love* is a heart-warming, captivating tale surrounding two souls who overcome the odds stacked against them and learn what it means to truly love. With humorous banter, vivid imagery, and an *Arabian Nights* vibe, Anna packs this novella full with important life lessons and themes that any reader can connect to and resonate with."

—DREW TAYLOR, author of *The Politics Of...* series and *The Designated* series.

"A beautiful combination of timeless love story, *Arabian Nights*, with a dash of realistic heartache, *By Light and Love* is a tale that lingers long after its finished."

—AJ SKELLY, bestselling author of *The Wolves of Rock Falls*, and *Magik Prep Academy* series

By Light and Love

Writing By Anna Augustine

Novels

When You Found Me

A Love Like Ours

Taletha

By Light & Love

By Blood & Blade

Anthologies

The Depths We'll Go To

Fool's Honor

Aphotic Love

Casting Call: Havok Season Six

A Taletha Novella

BY
Light
AND
Love

Quill & Flame
PUBLISHING HOUSE

ANNA AUGUSTINE

By Light and Love

Copyright © 2023 by Anna Augustine

Quill & Flame
PUBLISHING HOUSE

Published by Quill & Flame Publishing House, an imprint of Book Bash Media, LLC.

www.quillandflame.com

All rights reserved.

No part of this publication may be reproduced, digitally, stored, or transmitted in any form without written permission from the publisher, except as permitted by U.S. copyright law.

This is a work of fiction. Names, characters, and incidents are products of the author's imagination or are used ficticiously. Any similarity to actual people, living or dead, organizations, business establishments, and/or events is purely coincidental.

Cover design by Emilie Haney, www.EAHCreative.com

Internal Artwork Copyright © 2022 Dawn Davidson

Cover design by Emilie Haney, www.EAHCreative.com

Dedicated to my dear friends Nate and Anna.

Thank you for always encouraging me to keep pursuing my dreams.

Without you, none of my books would exist in physical form.

Rana
Mordova
capitol of Taletha
Saleem
Hasan
Taletha
Zara
Nasaria
The Nort Sea
Šeri
home of the Tribesmen

e Palace of
he Malek
Lower City
Middle City
High City

GLOSSARY

Cast of Characters

Saif of Mordova — (SAY-F) first born son of Sarju the Merchant

Saif's Family

Sarju the Merchant — (SAR-ju) Saif's father

Qamar of Rana — (QUA-mar) Saif's adoptive mother

Asim — (AH-sim) Saif's twin brother

Aisha — (AY-a-sha) Saif's half-sister

Bashar — (BAA-sh-AR) Saif's half-brother

Nafia — (NA-fee-a) Saif's half-sister

Ravi — (ra-VEE) intended of Saif's sister, Aisha

Ranya of Mordova — (RAY-na) a young woman from the lower level of Mordova

Ranya's Family

Majid — (MA-jeed) Ranya's oldest brother

Gazhi — (ga-ZEE) Ranya's younger brother

Janan — (JA-nan) Ranya's younger sister

Names & Titles

Ameer — Prince

Amira — Princess

Malek — King

Rania — Queen

Clothing

Kameez — An overdress that falls to the knees and has loose-fitting pants underneath

Kaftan — A long flowing dress with trailing sleeves

Kurta — A loose, collarless, long-sleeved, knee-length shirt worn by both men and women

Maang teeka — Head locket

Salwar — Cotton or silk pants worn under a kameez or kurta

Food

Baklava—Layered pastry dessert made of filo pastry filled with chopped nuts and sweetened with syrup or honey

Falafel—Balls of cooked chickpeas, usually fried in oil and flavored with garlic/onion, cumin, coriander, and pepper

Foul—A dip made with fava beans, typically flavored with garlic, lemon juice, tomato, onions, and parsley

Kofta—Balls of minced lamb or beef with a spicy onion kick

Manakeesh—Flat bread with sauce, meats, cheese, and herbs

Samoon—A stone baked bread, brushed with egg whites and vinegar on top and typically served with jelly

Shawarma—A spicy, slow-roasted chicken and pita bread

CHAPTER ONE

Saif

My back ached as I straightened from the stall of day-old fruits. Sunlight filtered through the rainbow of blankets and rugs that fluttered from ropes strung between the buildings in this section of Mordova. Dust clung to the sweat on my forehead and trickled down my chest as I smoothed my calloused hands against my salwar. They came away filthier than before.

Weariness weighed on my chest. I hated most everything here in the slums. The cacophony of animals and people blurred with the never-ending chants of the priests in the centrally located temple. One of the golden holy houses graced every level of Mordova—but those within were far from righteous. I was certain Nicar—goddess of all—frowned upon the pompous arrogance our priests carried with them wherever they went and the acts they committed behind closed doors.

My attention was drawn up the street as the morning bell signaled the start of the workday. A flash of white caught my eye. The palace of Mordova. The three red domes glared against the blue of the sky, the golden swallow of the royal family perched atop the center dome to judge all those who lived within its city's walls. I found it strangely ironic that the poorest district butted up against the malek's whitewashed palace. There he sat in all his splendor while his people slaved and starved right outside his door.

I stood behind my stall, folding my arms across my chest as the street came to life. Men, women, children. All bustled to and fro, ready to seize the day with vigor, despite whatever circumstance they found themselves in.

The clothing was as varied as the people themselves. Some of the women wore kameez and salwar—knee length tunics with flowy pants that cuffed at the ankle. Others preferred kaftans—dresses with long, flowing sleeves and skirts that fell to the ankle. The men all wore kurtas—tunics that reached the knees—vests, and salwar.

Despite the dire straits of many on this street, the colors of the clothing never ceased to amaze me. I loved all the varying shades of red, orange, yellow, green, blue, and purple swirling about the roadways, as if a rainbow had come and kissed the earth. Some were bright, others more faded and worn, but it was all beautiful to me. A testament that no matter how far the people of Taletha fell, they fought on.

"Good morning, Saif!" a cheery voice greeted me.

I turned, a smile on my lips for Ranya as she skipped up. She had been a frequent customer of my little stall since I'd taken up management six months ago. She was short, barely reaching my elbow. Her wavy black hair was pulled back from her face by a blue headscarf. Faint freckles dotted her already tan cheeks, and when she smiled, I caught sight of the small gap between her teeth.

"A very good morning, now that you've reached my stall." A wink had Ranya's cheeks flushing. "What will it be today?"

Ranya scanned my produce: a few pomegranates which were a little past ripe, apricots with wrinkles on their yellow-orange skin, coconuts that may or may not be good once opened. A flush of my own, this one a result of embarrassment, crawled onto my cheeks. I should have been able to get better wares than this. But that wasn't my job. No, I was responsible for the well-being of another and only did this job for him.

"Three pomegranates please." Ranya smiled and I found myself returning it as I picked out the best-looking ones and placed them in her basket.

"Anything else?" I asked. No other customers were nearby, and I found myself wanting to remain in Ranya's company as long as possible. She'd been coming to my stall every day for the last six months and I gladly spent as much time with her as I could. I knew much about her: her favorite color was green, she always purchased at least one pomegranate, and her smile made mine appear of its own accord.

She twirled a loose strand of hair around her finger and grinned. "What, trying to take all my coins today, fruit boy?"

"Quality fare for quality coin." I winked. "Besides, I take payment in pretty smiles."

That darkened her cheeks to an attractive shade of red. I'd learned within the first week of her visits that compliments made Ranya blush, and thus it had been my goal since to earn at least one blush from the girl each day.

"Flirt," she accused now, not meeting my gaze.

I chuckled. "Always."

"Saif!" I flinched as my uncle roared my name, staggering out from the shack he considered a home. He was a hulking brute of a man. His face was narrow—all angles and hard lines. His eyes were bloodshot, his teeth half-rotten from the amount of alcohol he consumed, and his hands were balled at his sides as he glared at Ranya and me.

"You aren't to be fraternizing with the customers." All his words were slurred as he leaned against the doorframe of the shack, the neck of a bottle still clutched in his fist.

"I'm not fraternizing, Uncle." I moved to block Ranya from his wrath. "I was being friendly with a customer. There is a difference."

"Not at my booth there isn't." He staggered forward, and the smell of body odor and whiskey nearly gagged me. He pressed my back into the wood of the stall. "Send her on her way."

I raised a brow at him, not at all concerned for my safety. It would be easy to knock him out if it came to that; his reflexes would be slow. I hadn't trained in hopes of becoming a soldier for Taletha for nothing. "I will do no such thing. If you want coin to waste on your drinking, then you'll let me serve the girl. If you don't, then I'll leave right now."

"Why you little—" He swung at me, eyes unfocused and face growing red.

I ducked under his fist, slipping around the stall and grabbing a wide-eyed Ranya by the arm. "Run!"

I slid my hand down her arm and clasped her hand, weaving in and around animals and pedestrians. We quickly outpaced my uncle, and I pulled Ranya into a narrow alley to catch our breath. Though, judging by the smell, I wasn't sure this had been the best place to hide.

"That man is your uncle?" Ranya gasped, pressing a hand to her chest.

"Yes." Butterflies took to circling in my stomach as I realized she had yet to drop my hand.

"Does he beat you?" She tipped her head back to look at me. It bumped the stone wall behind her, and she winced, rubbing at the spot. "He seems to have a horrible temper."

"He does have a temper, and while he's tried to hit me, I'm a bit too fast for him." I smiled, one side of my mouth hitching higher than the other as I squeezed her hand. Though mine dwarfed hers in size, holding her hand felt right. Natural even. I realized I looked forward to her visits each day, to her brilliant smile and sassy conversation.

"I—didn't realize you had to deal with that." She looks back the way we came. "Do you live with him?"

I hesitated. No, I didn't live with Uncle. But telling her the truth of where I came from—who I was? That would open up a whole conversation I wasn't ready for, not when our friendship was only just beginning.

"No, I don't." I rubbed my hand against my short black hair. "But you don't need to worry, I have a safe place to spend my nights."

She smirked, her free hand settling on her waist. "Who said I was worried?"

"I—It sounded like you were." I cleared my throat.

"Well, I think you can take care of yourself, Saif." Ranya's eyes scanned me, from the top of my head down to my feet. Then she laughed, tugging me back out onto the street. "Come on, let's go to the fountain plaza."

The fountains sat between the middle and lower sections of Mordova. There were six of them in total. There were five pillars around the plaza, a half circle basin with water falling down like a waterfall attached to each. The pillars were decorated with mosaics of trees, mountains, deserts, skies, and seas. They created a hexagon, with the largest fountain bubbling in the center. A star made with all the fountains' colors spread outward from the central fountain.

I loved going there to pray to Nicar, enjoyed the singing of the water and the prayers of others who strolled through the plaza. And that was the problem.

"I have a better idea." I gripped her hand, pulling her down another alleyway. "What if I told you I could show you a view?"

"A view?" Ranya parroted, a skeptical look on her face. "What kind of view?"

I smiled over my shoulder. "Do you trust me?"

She hesitated, looking into my eyes. My heart leapt at the depth of emotion that shone in her eyes—eyes the color of amber with a hint of green around the irises. Ranya may have had a life of poverty, but her eyes sang of hope and light.

Perhaps it would be enough to convince my family.

"Do you trust me?" I asked again, giving her hand a squeeze.

"Yes." She eased closer. "I trust you, Saif."

My heart soared and a large grin split my face. That was enough for me. "Then come on. I have something to show you."

Chapter Two

Ranya

Saif wove between the buildings like one born a street rat. So many who lived in Mordova were classified as such. It was sickening to me. The sheer number of children running amuck in Mordova was enough to disgust most people.

Most being the operative word. The malek didn't care, and neither did the priests. Women and children were reduced to objects, bartered and sold to the highest bidders. While many of the elite groomed their daughters to be sold to our Wife Markets—places wealthy men would go to secure a spouse—there were also "lesser" markets. Those were dark places, filled with all sorts of evil men. Women and girls were purchased for brothels and harems, while young boys were bought as slaves. The customers and owners alike didn't care if their merchandise was sullied. It was a livestock auction, nothing more and nothing less.

I shivered as we squeezed between two narrow walls, the sun momentarily eclipsed by the bricks. Saif glanced over his shoulder, one of his dark brows raised. "Are you all right?"

"Yes, simply lost in thought."

His grip tightened and I smiled. Despite being a giant of a man, Saif was thoughtful and generous, quick to smile and even quicker to defend. His actions with his uncle this morning had softened my heart, and I realized I was falling for him. Melting like ice left in the desert sun. It scared me—a nervous thrill shooting sparks through my body. What did it mean, to truly fall in love with a man? I had been infatuated before, like any young girl. But what I sensed growing in my heart for Saif felt different, more sure and solid.

I tucked all these thoughts close to my chest as Saif stopped abruptly and turned to face me.

"Close your eyes," he ordered. It hurt my neck, but I craned it back to look up at his face and raise a brow. His smile grew at my unspoken question. "You said you trusted me."

I glowered at him, barely suppressing a smile as I did. With a roll of my eyes that set Saif chuckling, I let my eyes closed with a little shake of my head. "Happy?"

"Very." He took my other hand and guided me forward. My senses heightened without my vision. A musty smell permeated the air, and it was even cooler here than it had been between the walls.

Something soft brushed my hand and then we were walking up steps. Saif took his time, letting me feel each step with my sandaled foot before I moved up. My pulse rang in my ears as up and up we went. Where was he taking me? And why was I hoping this little outing would end with a kiss?

You barely know the man! my head argued. But my heart *thump thump*ed in nervous anticipation. Because, for all my teasing and mock skepticism, I did trust Saif. Nicar above, I would trust him with my life if it came to it, and I didn't even trust my family with that. I was the reliable one, the one who provided food and clothes for all my siblings when Majid was out gambling away what little he had earned. My trust wasn't easily given and yet Saif had already earned a part of it. That scared me more than all the new feelings he stirred within me.

"All right." Saif placed his hands on my shoulders, stopping me. The sun once more shown on my face. I could feel it. The sounds of the city sounded far away, and below us somehow. A songbird twittered merrily from above. My brows furrowed as I tried to puzzle out where we were. Saif laughed again. The sound traveled down the length of his arm and vibrated my shoulder, warming me through.

"You don't have to look so bewildered, Ranya," he said, laughing again when I wrinkled my nose. "Open your eyes."

The sight stole my breath, my words, and all rational thought.

We stood on the roof of a tall, dilapidated building. Old rugs and carpets littered the rooftop and revealed the source of the musty smell. Dusty, cracked jars lined the low lip of the roof, set here and there in no particular order. Cushions with half of their stuffing missing were strewn around a few low tables. Though it was in shambles, it vaguely reminded me of some of the alehouses my brother frequented, places I found him passed out most nights when he didn't return home.

Rather than tell Saif that particular of my life, I asked, "What is this place?"

"An old tavern and inn." Saif gestured out across the city. "The view enticed the original owners to buy. But few people in this area were able to afford such luxuries, and few of the middle city wished to venture into the lower. The owners soon closed it down. Now some of the local children play here, and a few of the homeless sleep in the lower levels. The owners either don't know or don't care."

The end of his explanation sounded as if he knew the owners. But surely not. He knew the streets of Taletha too well to not be a street rat like the rest of us, meaning he couldn't possibly know the people who owned the old house.

I eased closer to him and to the edge of the roof as I looked out over the city. It was dazzling in the early afternoon light. Even from where we stood in the lower city, the various shades of browns and tans seemed to gleam—as if the houses were carved from solid gold.

Further down the winding streets came the middle city, where there were white, red, and even a few blue painted homes. And if I squinted and focused very hard, I could see the high city as it gleamed on the horizon in all its splendor. I had never visited there; I would have been escorted straight to prison if I had. But I could imagine what it would look like, how beautifully crafted the homes would be, and how lovely the people living within.

To the east stood the six white domes that were the homes of the Lords of Mordova. They were imposing, sitting as they did along the curve of the eastern wall. They butted up to the lower, middle, and high districts. There were supposed to be two lords over each district; their jobs were to see to the needs of their region. But besides visiting the malek in his palace, the lords rarely ventured out. They didn't care for anything except themselves.

"What do you think?" Saif asked, slipping his hand into mine once more.

"It's stunning," I answered honestly. "Thank you for bringing me up here. It's like seeing Mordova in a new light. As if it were a new world."

"Sometimes I wish I could make it new." He sighed, rubbing his hand over his short-cropped hair. "This city is so..." He waved his hand in a circle, as if he couldn't think of a word strong enough.

"It's stifling. Like you're running but not moving." I swallowed, visions of home and what waited for me there nearly choking me. "But it's the lot we've been given. What are we to do?"

"What if you could change your lot? Be someone else?" Saif's question had me looking up at him. The sun gleamed off his dark skin, accentuating his high cheek bones and square jaw. His large hand cupped the back of his neck as he stared out over the city. There was something about the way his jaw tensed, the way his shoulders rippled with tautness, that had my heart racing. What was he asking me? Was there a hidden meaning in his question?

Before I could voice my confusion, he turned toward me. His gaze was searing, like grabbing the handle of a pot hanging over the fire. And when it met my own, it seemed to brand my very soul.

I suddenly felt shy as Saif's hand tightened around mine and he stepped closer. He had to crane his neck down to look at me, and though he towered over me, I didn't feel frightened. My heart sped with excitement, hopeful that Saif might just kiss me after all. He picked up my other hand and asked, "If you had the chance to jump into a different life, would you?"

"It would depend," I whispered, somehow keeping it steady.

Saif managed to dip his head lower. He matched my whisper when he asked, "On what?"

"On who was jumping with me." Feeling the slightest bit daring, I stepped closer, our bodies nearly flush. I'd never been this close to any man—not even my father, Nicar rest his soul—and yet it felt incredibly *right* to be this near Saif. As if his arms were where I was meant to be.

My lips turned up ever so slightly as I heard Saif's sharp intake of air. His forehead brushed mine, then his nose rubbed against it. His head angled, and our lips were a mere hair's breadth apart when the temple bells chimed. We both jumped, our heads colliding, and hurriedly stepped apart.

"Are you all right?" Saif asked, his fingers brushing against his bruised brow.

"I'm fine." I forced a smile, though I was incredibly irritated. *Curse those stupid bells,* I thought darkly.

"I'd best get you back. I'm sure you'll have people looking for you if we stay away much longer?" He phrased it like a question, yet I deigned no reply. I might have found this boy to be attractive and chivalrous—might even be falling for him. But that didn't mean I was going to tell him about my sordid family and the life I was forced to endure.

CHAPTER THREE

Saif

Ranya was nearly silent as we wove our way back down the winding alleyways and sideroads of Mordova. I glanced over at her a number of times, a thought nagging me that I should walk her home. All the way home. See where she lived. Why had the mention of her family caused her to wall herself off tighter than the malek's palace?

I rubbed the back of my neck, fighting with myself as we neared my uncle's road. Was it an invasion of her privacy? I'd known her for six months. Yet over the last three, Ranya had become the bright spot in my day—the reason I even worked for my uncle at all. She was what made slaving over the pathetically lacking fruit booth worth my time and effort. And if I were being honest with myself, Ranya was the reason I was no longer quite so in love with the life I'd been born into.

Because it's not worth it if Ranya isn't there.

I gulped, panic clutching my throat. I was fairly certain Father would not be pleased if he knew who I had fallen for. And I knew without a doubt my twin, Asim, would have plenty to say. But one look at Ranya, and I knew I couldn't live without her, didn't want to live without her.

And it terrified me to no end.

"Ranya?" I paused in the road.

She took a few steps forward before glancing over her shoulder. A peculiar look must have been on my face because her brows lowered. "What's wrong?"

"May I—would you allow me to—?" My tongue felt five sizes too big for my mouth and my thoughts had all taken flight. I rubbed the back of my neck vigorously and then wiped my hand over my face before spitting out, "Can I walk you home?"

Ranya's mouth parted, her eyes widening. She said nothing for several seconds, dumbstruck by my question although I wasn't certain why. At last, she shook her head with a nervous giggle. "You wouldn't want to see my home."

"Wouldn't I?" I ate up the distance between us. Heat swirled in my gut when I picked up her hand, standing closer than was probably proper. The memory of our moment on the rooftop was still fresh in my mind. I had been so close to kissing her, so close to showing her I cared. Thank Nicar the bells of the temple had rung when they did, breaking us apart. If I were going to kiss Ranya, it would be because I was going to marry her. I wouldn't play with her heart. She would know the truth of who I was, and she would have the right to say yes or no without any deceit between us.

Ranya stared down at our hands and heaved a sigh. "No, you wouldn't. Please, go back to your uncle. I'll see you tomorrow."

With that, Ranya pulled her hand free from mine and left me standing in the street.

I had half a mind to follow her and see where she ended up, but the rational part of my mind told me it wouldn't be a good way to earn her trust. Enough deceit lay between us already. I wouldn't add to it by trailing her to her home.

With weary steps, I trudged back to my uncle's house. The stall had been picked clean of all its product. A stall left unattended was free for the taking, and the street rats had certainly seen to that. I smiled when I caught sight of two small children huddled in an alley, picking at the seeds of a pomegranate with giant grins on their faces.

I couldn't be upset by the loss. Not when it meant children had food in their bellies and smiles on their faces. It wasn't as if it were a loss to me. It wasn't even a loss to my father, as the fruit would have been tossed out regardless.

No, my father, Sarju of Mordova, was a fruit merchant. He had dozens of men working for him, groves upon groves of fruit trees outside the city, and we were seated quite comfortably as one of the head families of the middle city. What he wasn't able to sell in the first two days, he gave to his brother, my uncle. I had been told to sell it, the meager profits going to pay for my uncle's home and his ale. While I wasn't entirely thrilled with the job, getting to know Ranya had been an exciting and lovely benefit. It also meant being outside and away from parchment and figures and Asim.

I cleaned up the booth, ignoring the children all around eating my wares, before ducking under the old, threadbare tapestry to check on my uncle.

He was passed out on the floor, snoring loudly in the filthy hovel he called a home. Empty bottles covered every surface: the floor, tables, any level shelves on the wall. A horrible odor clung to the room, one-part unwashed body and the other human waste. I gagged and tried not to breathe as I dragged my uncle to his bed of ratty pillows and blankets in the corner.

Something scurried across the floor, and I didn't wait to discover what it was before ducking back out into the fresh air. The shadows were lengthening, the traffic thinning, as I began to trudge back toward my home in the middle city.

I might have looked out of place in my work clothes if it weren't for the other laborers and peddlers who frequented my part of Mordova. Their clothes were as varied here as they were in the lower levels. Turbans and veils bobbed alongside fezzes and kerchiefs. Coins jingled from pockets and jewelry alike. Bells rang on shoes.

From the plain brown tunics of the average house servant, to the ostentatious and outlandish garb of the peddlers, it was a swirling pool of classes, rank, and wealth.

Ducking between bodies and around carts and stalls, I soon reached the fountain plaza. The din of people lessened here. It had come to be a haven for me, a retreat from my two conflicting worlds and the reason I hadn't wanted to bring Ranya here. The tiles gleamed in the late afternoon light, and my eye caught the green and white ones adorning the fountain of petition.

I knelt before the fountain as it gurgled and splashed into the basin. Clasping my hands against the edge, I traced the mosaic pattern with my eyes as I began my prayer.

Nicar, goddess of all. I paused as I studied the tree. Its branches reached up into the sky, a reminder of how our prayers rose up to Nicar. All we had to do was beseech her. But what did I desire from the goddess? What did I truly want?

A few droplets of water splashed against my brow, cool and refreshing. My mind went to Ranya, the way her words and smile were equally as reviving as the water of the fountain. I looked up at the mosaic once more.

Nicar, goddess of all, I pray you would make a way for Ranya and I to be together. I fear my family will not like her simply because she was born in the lower levels. The prejudice against our people—who are the same as us in all but material wealth—must stop. I beseech you, please bring a way for it to cease. Make a way for Ranya and I to be together. Give us a way to bridge the lower and middle levels.

I sighed, stood, and rubbed the back of my neck. In so many ways, my prayer seemed impossible. Why would Nicar want to help me? I wasn't a particularly devout follower. I went to the temple once in a while to make a sacrifice and while I prayed frequently, especially here in the fountain plaza, it often felt like a useless endeavor.

Staring down into the frothing water, a single question floated through my mind. It breezed by so impossibly soft, I almost missed it. I glanced around for the person who had spoken, but the plaza was empty.

My mouth fell open in surprise before I grabbed hold of the whispered words.

What are you willing to give up to be with the one you love?

I looked up at the sky of orange, yellow, and pink and swallowed hard. *Is this from you?* I questioned.

But the plaza remained silent. No more strange questions wafted on the breeze. Rather, the scent of shawarma and manakeesh had me turning and hurrying for home.

A weight lifted off my shoulders as my house came into view. On the very edge of the high and middle levels, it was a three-level sandstone that towered over the squatter two level homes all around us. Five scalloped, horseshoe arched windows stretched across the uppermost levels, letting breezes blow through the bedrooms during the warmest parts of the days.

I stepped up to the large double doors and paused by one of the windows. Whitewashed lattice with circular patterns etched into it covered the four ground floor windows and offset the sandy brown of the rest of the house. Splashes of turquoise paint made geometric patterns around the window frames, lending a sophisticated air to our home.

Laughter and chatter came from inside—a typical night at our house. I could hear Aisha talking a mile a minute and it brought a grin to my face despite the exhaustion beginning to press down on me.

A low rumble of laughter raced through the air. Ravi, Aisha's betrothed, was visiting. Was he finally going to declare a wedding date? That would explain the excited chatter of Nafia and Bashar—my eleven-year-old sister and thirteen-year-old brother.

The only voices I didn't hear were Father's and Asim's. Anxiety swirled in my stomach as I stepped inside the doors and into the courtyard. Asim had wanted to take over the business for years—and he had a legitimate claim, being my twin. I was older by a mere ten minutes. It had been a constant worry for me that, because I didn't enjoy it like Asim did, he would inherit the business. Though, I'd often wondered if my future lay elsewhere in Mordova and not in fruits.

A squeal greeted me. I barely had time to brace myself before Nafia launched herself into my arms.

"Saif is home!" she hollered, making my ear ring from the volume.

I rubbed it against my shoulder and pretended to scowl at her. "And now he can't hear, Nafia! Thank you very much."

She giggled, hugging me tightly as I spun her in a circle before setting her back on her own two feet. The entire family gathered around me, all talking at once and making my head spin with the cacophony.

Aisha held out her hand, showing me a ring bearing a sparkling black diamond. Her smile looked almost painful. "The date is set, Saif!"

I smiled, though I was barely registering her words. "Congratulations, sister."

Ravi's arm was around her waist, his grin nearly as wide as Aisha. I clasped him on the shoulder and wagged a finger in his face. "You take care of her. The family of Sarju of Mordova fights for their own."

"Don't I know it!" Ravi laughed. "Do you know how intimidating you and Asim are? You're almost worse than your father."

The squeals and conversation picked up once more, nearly deafening in its exuberance. My day had been a whirlwind of emotions and adventures and all I wanted was some food and time to sort through everything that had happened. Particularly the strange question I had heard. As the volume continued to grow, I no longer had a clue what anyone was saying. Raising my hands, I tried to signal for silence, but it did little to staunch the noise. A piercing whistle rang out and the following silence was instantaneous.

"Why are you bombarding the boy the minute he walks through the door?" Father demanded. While he sounded angry, his black beard was unable to hide his beaming face.

"There you are, Sarju." Mother—who had simply stood back and watched her children chatter around me—tsked her tongue and stepped over to wrap her arm around Father's waist. "Where did you and Asim run off to?"

My twin's brown eyes danced with laughter as he came around to mother's other side and kissed her forehead. "We had some business to attend to."

Father's gaze cut to me, his black brow rising in question. "How was your day, Saif?"

I rubbed the back of my neck and shrugged. Father's forehead wrinkled, and he jerked his head for me to follow him to his study.

A sigh slipped free from Mother. "Now, Sarju? Truly?"

"I'll have the servants bring him some food."

"I haven't seen Saif since last evening." Mother crossed her arms and glared at Father. Only Qamar of Mordova could get away with scowling at my father.

But he took it with grace, smiling and pressing a kiss to her temple. "I shall endeavor to return him to you soon, my dear."

That seemed to pacify her. She gathered the rest of the family together and herded them over to the low table set up in the courtyard. She was a treasure, a gift to my father from the goddess herself, he claimed. I didn't doubt it for a moment.

I followed Father up the stairs that ran around the central courtyard. The whitewashed wood gleamed in the dying sun. Torches of lemon oil were being lit by the servants to ward off the evening insects as we hurried along to his office.

He closed the door behind us as I lowered myself down onto a red cushion with a sigh of relief. "It's been a long day, Father. I'm exhausted."

"What happened?"

I quickly told him about having to run from Uncle and protecting Ranya. I left out the near kiss in our old inn and alehouse, however. It wasn't a detail that was necessary for him to know. Not yet, at least.

Father swore. "He never was able to control himself, was he?"

It didn't seem like the type of question needing my response, so I kept silent.

"I assume the produce was gone by the time you returned?" Father asked, stroking his beard.

"Yes." The happy faces of the children filled my mind and I said, "We had many satisfied customers."

"Street rats get what they can, I suppose."

I bristled at the name. *Street rats.* It seemed so crass. I knew people saw me as one when I was in the lower city, and it chaffed. Why should those down on their luck be treated as less? It was wrong and ill-mannered. Ranya wasn't less than. She was life and light and—

"What else?" Father's voice shook me from my musings.

"There's nothing more."

"What was that?" Father gestured to his face with his index finger and raised a brow. "I know that look, Saif. Don't try to deny it."

"Deny what?" Panic clutched my throat. What had my expression given away?

Father laughed, slapping his leg. "Asim was right about you. There *is* a girl! Who is she?"

Asim knows about Ranya? My airway closed off completely, and I couldn't form a cohesive thought, let alone force words from my mouth. *Is this where I lose my family?*

CHAPTER FOUR

Ranya

I should have had Saif walk me home, I thought as the shouting reached me a block from my house. Majid was there, probably drunk out of his mind and in another fit of rage. But I had to go in. Hugging my arms to my chest, I stepped inside the one room hovel that was home.

The first thing I noticed was my younger brother and sister—Gazhi and Janan—huddled in the corner by the fireplace. Their eyes were round and when they saw me, they immediately rushed to my side and buried their faces against my kaftan. Their thin bodies trembled and my jaw clenched as another shout of anger rang around the room.

"Where have you been, you useless girl?" Majid roared. His towering frame barreled toward me, grabbing me by the arm and ripping me away from Gazhi and Janan. Gazhi cried out and Majid backhanded him, sending him sprawling into Janan.

"Leave them alone, Majid!" I struggled against his grip, but he simply tightened it, digging his fingers into my bicep. His breath reeked of ale, his face was haggard, and his brown eyes were bloodshot. No shirt covered his chest and sweat clung to it as if he'd run all the way home. He might have if he'd worn out his welcome at an ale or gambling house.

"Where were you?" he hissed.

"The bazaar." I gasped as he flung me into the wall. Shutting off my emotions, I braced for a beating. It wasn't the first time I had to suffer under my brother's hand, and I knew it wouldn't be the last. I would take a million beatings for Gazhi and Janan if it meant I could keep them safe. It was worth it.

But instead of his fist, Majid trailed his fingers over my cheek. "You're beautiful, Ranya."

Had he really said that? I jerked away from his hand and my chest tightened when he smiled lewdly at me. His eyes flicked over my body, and I hugged my arms against my chest to shield myself from his gaze.

"Why should that matter to you?" I whispered, scared of his answer.

"I need money." He leaned closer. "You'll bring me a lot of it."

I struggled to swallow, fought for air. "What do you mean?"

"The Market, dear sister!" He stepped back and strutted around the upended table with his arms outstretched. He looked like a peacock; far too much arrogance rolled off of him for one so drunk. "Tomorrow, you're going to be sold to the Wife Market to pay my debts."

The Wife Market. Not the one in the elite sector of Mordova, that was certain. With Majid as the seller, I'd undoubtedly be sold to a lesser Market. I would become a prostitute or a concubine to entertain men upon men, to be looked upon like a piece of meat rather than a woman with a heart and soul. And my own brother would be the one to subject me to that fate.

"You can't sell me." I shook my head vehemently. "I'm your sister. I'm the one who's keeping a roof over your head. I feed Gazhi and Janan. I shop and cook. You won't survive a day without me."

"Big talk for such a little girl." He stalked forward again, pinning me easily against the wall with his arm pressed up against my throat. "But who's going to save you? To the rest of Mordova, we're nothing but lower city gutter trash. Who would want you?"

Who indeed? It wasn't as if I had a line of suitors waiting for me. I was alone. It was my siblings and me against the world, and at that moment, the world was winning.

I swallowed my fear and met my brother's gaze. "Someday, someone will want me, Majid. He will love me and protect me and—"

The slap rang out loudly in the room, cutting off my words. I tasted blood on my tongue and tears blurred my vision as everything fell silent. Majid drew in great heaves of air. His pupils were large, his eyes unfocused as he stared at me. My brother hadn't seen me in ages, didn't see that he was losing the only family he had left because of how he treated us. I wanted to cry, my heart aching more than my cheek. How could anyone claim to love their family and treat them like this?

"Clean up this mess," Majid gasped at last as he gestured to the chaos he'd made in the room. I nodded, not meeting his gaze as he tumbled into bed along the far wall. Soon his snores filled the small space as he fell into a drunken slumber.

It took Janan, Gazhi, and me little time to clean up the room. We'd long ago given up owning any pottery or things that could be smashed against the sandstone walls. Righting the table, we resituated our cushions and blankets by the hearth, the low embers of the fire warming our trembling bodies as we curled up together.

"You're not going to let him sell you, are you?" Gazhi asked in a whisper, his large eyes wide in his tan face. His long curls fell in his eyes and I smoothed them away as Janan snuggled up against my back. Her silent tears soaked through my threadbare kaftan and she hugged my waist with her thin arms, as if her will alone could keep me with them.

I longed for words of comfort, something to reassure them that I wasn't leaving. But I wasn't certain there was a way out. Majid was our guardian, the one supposedly responsible for protecting us. Tears clouded my vision and I choked back a sob. What was a person supposed to do when their shield became the very thing that was attacking them?

Nicar above, please send someone to protect us.

Saif's face floated across my thoughts and a soft voice whispered, "Go to him."

"I will," I muttered as a restless slumber finally claimed me.

CHAPTER FIVE

Saif

Father laughed at my speechless expression and again asked, "Who is she?"

I shook my head.

Father's smile vanished and he raised his brow. "Listen, boy, I told you not to lie to me. I know there's a girl. Who is she? To which family does she belong?"

Air finally filled my lungs and with it, the words snapped into place. "She's not someone you'd approve of, Father. She's from the lower city."

"And why do you think I wouldn't approve of that?"

I blinked. "You've worked so hard for what we have. I didn't think you'd want me to throw it away on a lower city girl."

My father snorted—a sound I'd never heard him make before—and shook his head. "Then you don't know me at all, my son. Do you love her?"

I shrugged. "I—"

Father held up his hand. "And if you don't know now, do you think you could fall in love with her?"

"Love?" I rubbed my neck.

"Talk it out with me." Father crossed his arms and leaned against the wall. His eyes closed and he gestured for me to process my thoughts out loud. I'd always been one who had to talk out my problems. Asim, he could think through them and arrive at a conclusion on his own. But not me.

With a sigh of frustration, I began. "Ranya has been coming to the stall for six months."

"So since you started?" Father questioned.

"Yes." I cupped my chin in my hand, resting it on my knees. "And every time I've thought of her over the last few weeks, it brings a smile to my face. I realized today that she makes my pathetic job of selling fruit for Uncle worth it. I hate the stall, the street, the smells. It reminds me of everything wrong in our world. But seeing her smile, listening to a story from her, it makes my day better. When she arrives at my stand, I find I can breathe a little easier, smile a little wider. Life is better when she's there."

"She sounds like a special girl," Father noted, cracking open one eye and smiling knowingly.

I shook my head. "But is she the right one?"

"That's a choice only you can make, Saif." Father leaned forward and clasped my shoulder. "Listen, son. You know my life, my choices. No two paths are ever the same, yet I see so much of myself in you. Whether or not this girl is the *one* is up to you to decide. Because that's what love is, a choice. But I want you to know that I will support you if you choose to pursue her. Regardless of her past, she can have a future with us."

I smiled, but it felt wobbly. The adrenaline from the day began to press down on me, and I wanted nothing more than to sink into the oblivion of sleep. "Father, how did you know Mother was the one?

"It was that I felt more like myself with her than anyone else. That I was free to feel and think and I wasn't judged." He got a faraway look in his eyes. "Qamar is the same way."

The veins in my temples pounded, the pain making my stomach turn. "Do you mind terribly if I go to bed?"

"I don't," Father lowered his voice, "but your mother might."

A chuckle tinged with exhaustion escaped. I felt weary in my very bones.

Father must have heard it, for he gestured toward the door. "Go to bed. I'll smooth things over with your mother."

"Thank you, Father. For everything."

"Of course, my boy." He pulled me into a quick embrace, smacking my back twice before pushing me toward the door. "Rest well."

I staggered into my room, throwing off my dirty clothes and tumbling into my bed with a groan. The sheets were cool and smelled of lavender. The scent tugged my eyelids closed with a sigh. As I drifted off to sleep, the question came again.

What are you willing to give up to be with the one you love?

Morning came far too soon, and with it the fear of my decision. While Father supported me, there were still Mother and Asim. Could I marry a lower city girl without their blessing?

"I could always bring her to visit," I said to myself as I dressed in clean, but worn, salwar and kurta. "She could find out about my life and family and I can see Mother and Asim with her."

I rubbed my neck. Was that a wise idea? Perhaps I should tell Ranya about my life *before* dropping her in the middle of it all.

"Nicar above, this is difficult," I grumbled as I thumped down the stairs to the courtyard and breakfast.

Mother and Father were already at the table, talking in low voices as I sat across from them. Foul, hummus, pita bread, and falafel graced the table. I took a generous helping of it all.

As I began to eat, both of my parents turned to study me with curious expressions on their faces.

"What?" I asked after I swallowed a mouthful of foul and pita bread. It was hard not to squirm under their scrutiny.

"You're right, my dear," Mother stated as she patted Father's cheek, grinning at me. "He has all the signs."

"Signs of what?" I asked, slight exasperation huffing out on a sigh.

"You're in love." Mother reached across the table and clasped my hand. "I may not be your mother by blood, but I raised you as my own. I know you, Saif."

That she does. Qamar had raised Asim and me since the day we were born. We'd never known our real mother as she'd passed giving us life. Father talked about her often, his love for our birth mother evident even now. Qamar had come to be our wet nurse, even though she'd been from the lower city. She had cared for and loved us all our lives. When we had turned one, Father had married her, as drawn to her as we were. I couldn't believe that I had forgotten such an important part of our family history. Why had I doubted that she would understand?

"I think I may be falling in love," I admitted. "But she's from the lower city and I fear—"

"Fear has no place with love, my son." Mother's brows rose. "Love looks at the impossible and says, 'I will leap'. It looks at a horrible mess and says, 'I will make a masterpiece from the chaos'. It looks at the rain and says, 'this will create a beautiful garden'."

"But what if she's not the one?"

"Did you hear nothing I told you last night?" Father sighed and heaved his eyes skyward. "Nicar help us with this one."

Mother swatted his arm, eliciting a chuckle from Father, before she turned back to me. "Saif, I am a firm believer that love is a choice. Your father loved your mother. Loved her even when he married me. But we had to choose to love each other through the highs and lows of raising you and Asim, having the rest of your siblings, growing his business. Love grows stronger through the hard times, through the challenges. The trick is to continue to choose love, no matter what."

I looked down at my half-finished plate, contemplating her words. My parents were silent, watching me with a mixture of pride and love on their faces. Could I do it? Could I choose Ranya day in and day out for the rest of my life? When we grew haggard and gray, would I still pick love over resentment? When hard times happened, when we had to fight for love and laughter, would I pick her again? I closed my eyes, seeing her smile and hearing her laugh, feeling the spark of light that shined out of her despite a life in the lower city.

What are you willing to give up to be with the one you love?

After giving me a moment, Mother said, "I don't wish to talk you to death, Saif. You're a man now, capable of making your own choices. We trust you to make the right one. Whomever you marry will be blessed indeed to call you her husband."

I nodded.

"Now get to your stall." Father winked, wrapping an arm around Mother. "You're going to be late opening if you don't."

"Yes, Father." I kissed Mother's forehead before striding out the door and toward Uncle's house. All the way, their words wove through my mind.

Love is a choice.

Fear has no place in love.

You will make the right choice.

I sighed as I reached the fountains, dropping down before the fountain of petition yet again. *Nicar above, I need your wisdom.*

Leaning my forehead against the basin, I poured out all my confusion. I wasn't sure what the right choice was, wasn't sure where a relationship with Ranya would lead, or if it was even right to pull her into one.

What are you willing to give up to be with the one you love?

Peace surrounded my heart when I finally admitted the thought that had been hovering on the edges of my consciousness since the day before.

Everything. I'm willing to give up everything to be with Ranya.

Pushing to my feet, I ran to my stall. I wove between the children along the streets, around the few peddlers and merchants already up, before skidding to a stop by my stall. I hurried to unload the crates of old fruit. Finishing in record time, I began to pace before my booth, wondering what in the world I would say to the woman I wanted to be my wife.

Chapter Six

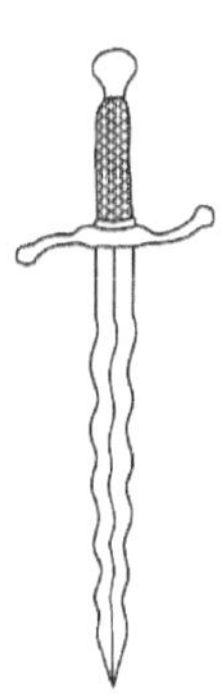

Ranya

The sun had barely risen by the time I hurried Gazhi and Janan out the door. Majid still slumbered on his bed, and there wasn't a chance on earth I was leaving my siblings with him after the drunken rage he'd been in the night before. Visions of what he might do to them choked the air from my lungs as we marched down the street, their hands gripped tightly in my own.

"Where are we going?" Gazhi asked, a spring in his step as we hurried past the brothels and ale houses that lined our sordid street. No one was awake, still sleeping off whatever revelry they'd enjoyed the night before—whether it was women, alcohol, or a bit of both.

"To visit a friend of mine," I replied, skirting a puddle of vomit.

Janan raised a brow. "Is this person safe?"

I smoothed my thumb over the back of her hand and tried to smile reassuringly. "He's trustworthy, Janan. Trust me."

She eased closer. "I trust *you*; it's everyone else who's the problem."

My heart ached at the bitterness in my sister's voice. She was only ten years old and already had a tainted view of the world. No child should fear her own brother, worry about being sold for her body, flinch at any raised voice. But that was our life, and I couldn't change it any more than I could change the direction of the wind.

We turned the corner to the bazaar. Quilts and garments fluttered on the lines, filling the street with wild colors and casting shadows in the new daylight. This street, while still cramped and crowded, felt cleaner and safer than ours. A few merchants and peddlers were up, setting up their wares and shouting greetings to one another as I hustled Gazhi and Janan toward Saif's uncle's house. I wondered if his uncle would be angry to see me again. But I had no choice. I needed help and somehow, I trusted Saif to give it to me.

The house and stall came into view and with it Saif, pacing before his booth. His black brows were furrowed, his lips moving as if he were muttering to himself. I began to quicken my steps, but both my siblings dug in their heels.

"*That's* your friend?" Gazhi's already large eyes nearly doubled in size. "He's a giant!"

"He's not that big," I denied, but a glance over my shoulder made me realize how towering Saif really was. "He's been a good friend to me."

"Do you really trust him, Ranya? Really, really trust him?" Janan asked, watching Saif with a doubtful expression.

"Yes, Janan. I trust him with my most precious treasures." I waited for them to look at me. "I trust him with you. He will keep us all safe and protected."

"Do you think Majid will try to hurt us?" Gazhi asked, burying his face into my kaftan when I nodded.

Janan glared at Saif's back before sighing. "All right, then. If you trust him, so do I."

I smiled and slowly led them toward Saif. What would he think when he saw me with my siblings? Would he still smile and greet me the way he always did? What about our near kiss? Was it all in my head, or was he truly interested in me? What would it mean if he *was* interested? Could he protect me from Majid?

"Good morning, Saif." My voice quavered ever so slightly with the onslaught of worry flying through my mind. I coughed to clear the lump in my throat.

"Good morning, Ranya." He turned toward me, a shy smile on his face as he met my gaze. I blinked, confused as to why he would feel shy after nearly kissing me the day before. Heat climbed into my cheeks as his gaze moved to Gazhi and then Janan. He raised a brow. "And who are these fine-looking children?"

"This is Gazhi and Janan. They're my siblings."

Tears pricked my eyes as Saif knelt, smiling warmly at my brother and sister. "It is an honor to meet you both."

Janan inclined her head, the proper greeting for a man not related to her. I squeezed her hands encouragingly. Gazhi just stared at Saif, his mouth hanging half open before he said, "You're a giant!"

Mortification brought color into my cheeks, but Saif tipped his head back and laughed, his eyes sparkling when he looked at me and then back at Gazhi. "I am indeed. But you should see my brother Asim." His voice dropped to a loud whisper. "He's even taller than I am!"

Gazhi's mouth fell open completely and his eyes somehow grew larger still. "Can I meet him?"

"Gazhi, that isn't polite," I reprimanded, my blush darkening. My brother often forgot to think before he spoke.

"It's fine." Saif stood, his gaze fixated on my face. "I would like you to meet my family."

"Saif—" I squeezed my eyes shut. "Can we go somewhere and talk? I—"

When my voice cracked, Saif's brows lowered. "Is something wrong?"

I nodded, my throat too thick with emotion to say anything more.

"Are you in danger?" Saif's voice took on a dark tone and a shiver worked its way down my back.

When I still didn't reply, Janan nodded. "We all are."

"Janan." I shot her a warning look but Saif's hand on my shoulder had my gaze returning to him.

"Let's go to the old ale house." Saif scooped up Gazhi and settled him on his shoulder before slipping his hand into mine.

"What about your stall?" I asked. "You surely lost the produce yesterday. Can you afford—?"

"It's fine, Ranya. Trust me."

Trust. Why was that so hard for me? I wanted to take his hand and run away. Trust he would be there with me through it all. And while I trusted him to help me *now,* would he stay? Would he be the man I'd grown to know over the last six months or would he tire of me eventually and become like Majid?

We wove through the buildings, down the alleys and back streets until we reached the ale house. I hadn't realized the day before that it was on the very edge of the middle and lower cities. Its four stories towered above the houses and businesses all around it.

Saif swung Gazhi off his shoulders, pressing a hand against my back as he smiled down at my siblings. "Janan, why don't you and

Gazhi go up to the roof while I talk with Ranya? See what you can see from up there."

Janan glanced at me. When I nodded, she clasped Gazhi's hand and ducked under the old blanket shielding the door to the stairs without argument.

"What's wrong?" Saif asked the moment the children were gone.

"What's right?" I laughed mirthlessly. "I don't even know where to start."

Saif reached for my hands and I let him clasp them. "Janan said you were in danger. Danger from whom?"

"Our brother, Majid. He's a drunk and a gambler, and while he's always been abusive, last night he threatened to sell me to one of the Wife Markets."

Saif's grip on my hands tightened.

"It would be a lesser market and I don't—I can't—" A sob caught the end, and I pressed my lips together until I could speak again. "I didn't know who else to turn to."

"Oh, Ranya." He tugged me closer. I let myself crumple against his solid chest, let him wrap his strong arms around my back, and let myself fall apart in the safety of his embrace.

CHAPTER SEVEN

Saif

Ranya sobbed and I tightened my hold around her. Hatred for a man I'd never even met burned in my heart. How *dare* he make her cry like this! He would pay. I'd see to it myself if it came to that.

"Did he lay a hand on you?" I asked once her sobbing abated.

"He bruised my arm last night. Smacked my face. He pushed Gazhi into Janan, but it was too dark to see if he was injured last night and I didn't wait this morning to check."

I tucked a piece of her hair behind her ear, seeing a bruise against her cheekbone. It took biting the inside of my cheek to keep from swearing.

"This has happened before?" I asked as levelly as I could.

"Only when he's drunk. Though he's never—" she shivered "—he's never threatened to sell me before. That's why I came to you. I don't know what to do, Saif. I can't let him hurt Gazhi and Janan, and if I'm not there, he will."

With the passion and love burning in her gaze, she was breathtaking. And it was then that I knew, beyond a shadow of a doubt, that I *loved* this woman standing before me. Despite everything, she was still trying to carry herself with poise and grace and it floored me. Her beauty captivated me, but it was her heart that had won me completely. Her love, her light, her determination. It all poured out of her in a flood and was far sweeter than any honey.

Ranya looked up at me, tears wetting her lashes, and asked, "What am I going to do?"

She didn't know about my family yet, didn't know I had the money to buy her and her siblings' freedom from her brother. But it didn't matter to me. Even if I had been the poorest of the poor in Mordova, I would work until my hands and feet bled to rescue her. She was worth every ounce of discomfort, every drop of sweat, every tear.

I tipped her chin up from where she had buried it against my chest. Her curls were in disarray around her face today, rather than neatly pulled back. I tucked a stray one behind her ear, cupping her face with my palm after I finished. "Do you trust me?"

She nodded with a small sniff.

"Is it safe for you to return home?"

"He said he'd sell me this morning." Another sob caught in her throat and she laid her ice-cold fingers against my hand on her cheek. "I trust you, but I don't trust anyone else, least of all my brother."

Her distress flooded over me, causing tears of my own to prick my eyes. I pulled her close, and she came, grabbing a fistful of my kurta as muffled sobs shook her slim frame. A light breeze blew her curls in my face, their amber-scented strands caressing me with their softness. We stood there for what felt like an eternity—the most blessed minutes of my life.

"I'm terrified," she whispered as a faint strain of children's laughter carried down from the rooftop. "I want a family and love, Saif. If he sells me to the Market, I'll become a prostitute or a concubine or...worse."

"Ranya." The words stuck in my throat. So much to say, but was this right? Was now the time to tell her how I felt? Did I dare offer this when it might look like just a quick fix to her problem?

"What is it?" She stepped back, looking up at me, her light brown eyes gleaming in the sunshine. "What's wrong?"

"When we were here yesterday, I realized something." I swallowed, feeling far more flustered than I wanted. "I realized this before you came to the stall today, and I planned on saying this before your news, please know that."

"Saif, you're not making sense." Her brows puckered.

"I'm falling in love with you, Rayna." The words jumped out of my mouth before I could stop them, and I bit my tongue as they pranced in the silence between us.

Rayna's eyes widened, much like Gazhi's had as he stared up at me earlier. But where her brother's expression had made me smile, Ranya's expression had me squirming. After what felt like an eternity, she shook her head and whispered, "You can't mean that. Not now, not after what I told you. My family, my life, you can't want that, Saif."

"It was your confession about your life that showed me how much I've grown to love you. I want to protect you; I want to fight for love. I know you're scared, and this is rather sudden but—" I rubbed the back of my neck. "I'm choosing to love you, Ranya. Please, choose to love me, too."

Her eyes flicked between my own, her lips pursing into an *O* of confusion. "You love me?"

"Yes. Or at least, I'm beginning to." I clasped her hands and pulled her closer. "My mother told me that love is a choice. And when you came to me—terrified and with your family in tow—I knew I would move heaven and earth to protect you and them. It might not be love yet, but I want to grow to love you more each and every day."

"Saif—" She was shaking her head. "You can't mean that."

"Trust me, Ranya. Trust and jump with me." I dipped my head, pressing my forehead to her own. "Marry me, let me protect you from your brother. Let me take you home and meet my family. They'll adore Gazhi and Janan. Let me love you. Learn to love me with all my quirks and flaws. Let's make a masterpiece out of this mess. You and me against the world."

"Saif." She looked about ready to say no, ready to argue why it was a bad idea. She shook her head, but then her eyes dropped to my lips and then next thing I knew she was kissing me.

It was slight, barely there at all. She started to lean back but my hand slipped to her waist, drawing her closer, deeper. Her hands wrapped around my neck and she rose onto her tiptoes, pressing into me. It was fire and ice, untested and untried, but it was all the sweeter because of it.

She leaned back first, burying her nose into my neck. "I'm—I'm still not sure. What if you're wrong about us?"

"After that kiss?" I huffed out a laugh that was part frustration, part humor. "I'm more certain now than ever before."

She was silent, and I simply held her, cradling her like the precious treasure she was. Ranya had been ground to a pulp, like the grapes the vintners bought from us to turn to wine. Trodden under the feet of words and actions, she was wrung dry. There was still light and hope within her, but it was fragile, easily smothered.

A shudder raked her frame, and she tightened her hold on me. "If you want me, despite all the baggage that comes with me, I'll marry you, Saif."

I scooped her up and spun in a circle. "Yes. I wouldn't have asked you if I wasn't certain. I will give you a family and love, Ranya. Upon my word, I will."

A tear glistened on her cheek and I brushed it away with the pad of my thumb. My heart was both heavy and light. I was going to marry the woman I wanted to love for the rest of my life. Her pain made my chest ache. I couldn't imagine laying a finger on my brothers and sisters in anger. Yet there was a man in Mordova doing just that. Probably more than one.

I squeezed Ranya's hand and Pressed a kiss to the top of her head. "Let's get Gazhi and Janan. It's time for you to meet my family."

CHPATER EIGHT

Ranya

"Where are we going?" Gazhi asked. He was riding on Saif's shoulders once more, his skinny arm wrapped around the tall man's forehead.

"To my home." Saif squeezed my hand. "I live in the middle city."

I stopped abruptly, yanking my hand from Saif's. "We can't go there! We'll be arrested."

"Peddlers and merchants go through there all the time. The patrols know me. You'll be fine." His voice was low and soothing, as if he were trying to calm a wild animal.

"You don't know that. You don't know that you'll be able to protect us, or that the middle city will welcome us." I bristled and glared at him, causing Saif to raise his hands in defense.

"I know my parents will at the very least. They gave their blessing for me to pursue you, Ranya. And that's what this is. Pursuing." He raised his brows, his face asking me to trust him once more.

I don't like this, I thought, a war waging in my mind. I couldn't go back to Majid. He would sell me to support his indulgent lifestyle. It wasn't safe for Janan and Gazhi to be there either. For all that he was family, Majid hadn't the slightest bit of love in him. I wasn't even certain he knew what love was.

But did I dare trust the hulking giant at my side? I watched him, but he was listening to something Gazhi was saying with rapt attention. His eyes flicked to me and he raised his brow, the question of trust deep in his eyes. With a sigh, I slipped my hand back into his. I had trusted Saif, the lower city fruit merchant. Why should Saif the middle city citizen be any different?

An expression I couldn't identify flashed across Saif's face as he guided me down the road. It pinched at my heart, so much so that I found myself whispering, "Saif, is this really what you want?"

He stopped in the middle of the street, a grumble emanating from in his chest that sounded very much like a growl. Without warning, he turned me to face him and kissed me in front of my brother, sister, and all the people along the edge of the road. It was short, but the heat it sent through me made my head spin. He leaned back, a smile dancing around the corners of his mouth. I was breathless and wanted very much to pull him in for another mind-altering kiss.

"Does that answer your question, Ranya?" he asked in a husky whisper.

"Quite nicely, yes."

He laughed, tucking my arm into his before continuing to guide us down the road.

"Are you going to marry my sister?" Janan asked abruptly. She walked ahead of us a few steps and looked over her shoulder to glare at Saif. She still didn't trust him.

"Yes." Saif tugged me closer.

Janan glanced at me. "When?"

Saif cleared his throat. "Tonight, if she's willing."

"Tonight?" My voice cracked and my pulse began to thunder in my ears. The irrational part of me wanted to run from all of this, to run and not look back. Because why would Saif marry a girl from the lower city?

I tried to yank my hand out of his but Saif tightened his hold. "The sooner you marry me, the sooner I have a legitimate claim to protect you and your siblings from Majid."

At his words, Janan's eyes widen. "Marry him tonight, Ranya. You love him, he loves you, and it will protect us all from Majid."

"Janan, I don't—"

"You love him," she insisted, yanking my hand from Saif's and grabbing me by my forearms. "You look at him the way Momma used to look at Poppa."

She remembered that look? It was ingrained into my memories, but Janan had been eight when Momma and Poppa had died of some unknown sickness. That look was one of complete adoration and awe. It sprung to life on Momma's face when Poppa would play with us on the floor or read the sacred text before the fire at night. I'd seen it as they danced around our home to whatever tune Poppa hummed in Momma's ear and the strongest memory of all was of the swoony smile they both wore after a tender kiss. I'd caught it a few times, usually at night when they thought I was asleep. Did I look at Saif that way? Was I falling in love with him like he claimed he was with me?

"Ranya?" Janan shook me, her dark brown eyes full of pleading. "Please, marry Saif."

"I already said I would." I looked up at Saif, thankful to discover Gazhi was once again chattering—this time about the ornate houses that were appearing around us.

We began moving again. Saif was a few feet ahead and Janan threaded her arm with mine.

"You'll marry Saif tonight?" she persisted after a few minutes of walking.

"Janan, I don't know—"

"He's nice." Janan bit her lip. "He doesn't have that cruel gaze."

"What do you mean?" I peeled my eyes from Saif and Gazhi to watch my sister's face.

"When he smiles, it shines in his eyes. When he laughs, it's his whole body. It's not forced or fake." Janan shrugged. "Majid has had cruelty in him for a long time, since even before Momma and Poppa died."

I didn't have time to respond before Saif turned and gestured to a large, three-story house a few feet from us. "Welcome home, Ranya, Janan, and Gazhi."

Home. It looked too lavish, too pristine to be *our* home. I shook my head, letting my gaze travel over the light blue patterns, white lattice, and the many windows. Was this really my new reality? With vows to Saif, would I become a middle citizen?

"Ranya? Are you going to be all right?" Saif swung Gazhi off his shoulder and my brother clasped Janan's hand. I focused on them, unable to look up into Saif's face.

"I will be. It's simply...a lot to take in."

Saif tucked a finger under my chin and turned my face toward him. "No, something is bothering you. What is it?"

"You truly want to marry me?" Tears burned my eyes and I squeezed them shut, scared of what I'd see in Saif's gaze. "I'm a lower city citizen. You won't tire of me later?"

"Oh, Ranya." His thumb caressed my cheek. "If you don't want to get married tonight, we don't have to."

"Do you want me to marry you?" I forced myself to look at him.

Saif wore a half smile and nodded. "Yes. I already told you that."

"It's just all so sudden. I don't know—"

"I want you to be ready for this. For marriage and a life together. I don't want to rush you. But it will protect all of us more if we are wed."

My heart jumped into my throat. "Will you get in trouble for having my siblings in your house?"

"Possibly. But it's a risk I'm willing to take. Majid will *never* lay a hand on them or you again." Venom and steel laced Saif's words, and I found myself believing him.

"Would us being married protect them more?" I whispered, my body swaying closer to him of its own accord. *And you? Will it protect your reputation?*

"It would." He cupped my face with his large hands. "But what I'm more worried about is our hearts. I want to protect *them*, too. This isn't a decision I'm making lightly. Marrying you is forever with no backing out once everything is safe. If we make this sacred vow, it will be binding. I'm not leaving."

"You're a middle citizen." I leaned back to see his face fully once more. "Do you really want to marry a lesser citizen with two siblings in tow?"

"Nicar above, I've already told you the answer." He leaned his forehead against my and whispered, "*Yes.*"

Saif said it with such fervor that it stole any further arguments from my tongue. With a small smile, I wrapped my arms around his waist and buried my face against his chest, breathing him in. He smelled of lavender and something else I couldn't place—something fresh and new and exciting.

He curved his arm around my back and whispered against my hair. "As much as I love being able to hold you, I know my family is gawking at us from the courtyard. Are you ready to meet them?"

I stepped back, smoothing my trembling hands against my kaftan, feeling unkempt and dirty next to Saif's home. Would his family see me as worthy of their son and brother? Or would they find me as lacking as I found myself?

CHAPTER NINE

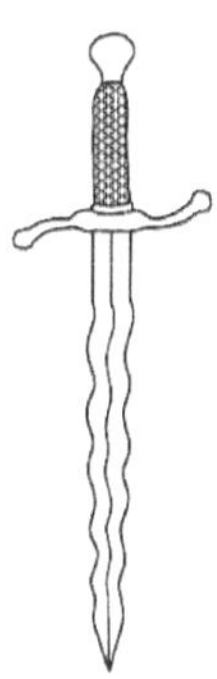

Saif

Ranya was nervous. I couldn't say I entirely blamed her as my nerves were wound a bit as well. Her eyes darted around as she quickly grabbed her sibling's hands in her own. I laid mine against the small of her back and guided them all toward the door.

"They will love you all," I promised, though I wondered what Asim would say. He hadn't been present with Mother and Father when they gave their blessing for me to pursue Ranya and I so desperately wanted my twin's approval. I always had. Even being the older one by birth, it seemed Asim was older at heart, more level-headed and confident in himself. I envied that. And perhaps that was the reason I strove to please him almost as much as I did my parents.

It didn't help that Asim and I had always been somewhat at odds. He wanted to run Father's business, but it was mine by right of birth. While I enjoyed the more social aspects of Father's merchant business, I didn't have the head for numbers that my brother did. And while running the fruit stall for my uncle, I'd come to discover the joy of working with my hands, of serving others and caring for the ones I loved. It felt good to earn my own merit.

"Are you certain this is wise?" Ranya asked as I set my hand on the latch. Her face was twisted into an expression of half fear and half uncertainty.

I brushed her hair off her shoulder and leaned close. "Very, very certain."

Ranya sucked in a sharp breath and giggled nervously.

Happy with my little triumph, I pressed a kiss to her cheek and swung open the door. "I'm back!"

The clatter of dishes sounded from the center of the courtyard and then Mother hurried forward. Her hair was done up tightly. The sweat on her brow and flour on her hands were testament to the fact that she'd been in the kitchens today, working her magic on a lump of dough. She swiped the back of her wrist against her forehead, leaving behind a trail of white, and grinned at Ranya and her siblings. "Welcome to our home! I'm Qamar, and we're so happy you're here."

"Th-thank you." Ranya glanced up at me, puzzlement outweighing the fear.

"Mother, this is Ranya, her brother, Gazhi, and sister, Janan." I lightly touched each of their shoulders with a smile, my eyes catching sight of the rest of the family around the table. "They may be staying with us for a while."

Mother's brows rose but she nodded. "Well, Ranya, Gazhi, and Janan, we are glad to have you with us." She smiled and gestured further into the courtyard. "Come meet the rest of the family."

I chuckled, my hand settling against Ranya's back once more. "You mean they weren't staring through the windows earlier?"

Mother scowled at me for the barest second before the corners of her lips rose. "Nafia might have been."

"Hello!" My sister sprung forward from her spot at the table and clasped Janan's hand. "I'm Nafia! I'm Saif's sister and am eleven. How old are you? Do you like dolls? I have a special glass doll Poppa traded for and she's my very best friend, but now you're here and we can be best friends, don't you think?"

"Nafia!" I laughed as she turned her large hazel eyes my way. "Breathe, sister."

She sucked in a breath and then continued rambling to the wide-eyed Janan, who merely followed after Nafia as she hauled her up the stairs to her room.

"And your name is Gazhi, right?" Mother knelt down to the boy's level. He still clung to Ranya's hand, his cheek pressed against her arm. When he nodded shyly, Mother said, "Well, Saif's brother,

Bashar, was telling us that his cat had kittens last night. Would you like to go see them?"

His eyes lit up, losing most of the glazed look they'd had since stepping through the door. He looked up at Ranya. "Can I?"

She smiled, but it was wobbly. "If you'd like."

He nodded and Bashar stepped forward with his crooked grin. "Come on, Gazhi! They're this way."

The eight-year-old trotted after my brother and disappeared into Bashar's room with the sweet refrains of chatter already starting.

"Now, you two." Mother stood and smiled at us. "I want to hear about everything."

Ranya eased closer to me, her arms crossing over her chest. "It's a long story."

"Well, we were getting ready to sit down to a meal. Are you hungry?"

Ranya's stomach chose that moment to growl loudly and a pretty blush bloomed in her cheeks.

Mother laughed. "I'll take that as a yes."

"We didn't have a chance to eat before leaving home this morning," Ranya admitted, her gaze traveling over the rest of the family with uncertainty.

"Well, then it's a good thing it's baking day in our home." Mother was already filling a plate with kofta, falafel, hummus, and fresh pita bread. She poured a goblet of spiced wine and sat it all before

Ranya and motioned for me to sit in Bashar's empty seat. "Now for you to meet the rest of the family."

I was truly impressed by my family's lack of chatter over introductions. As Mother presented each of the family to Ranya, I took stock of their expressions. Father had his chin cupped in his palm, watching the whole exchange with interest. Asim had a scowl on his face as he glared first at me, then Ranya with undisguised disgust. Aisha's brows were raised, and she kept leaning over to whisper in Ravi's ear.

"And that's everyone!" Mother sighed in contentment. "My large, wonderful family."

"Family is a blessing," Ranya stated, tracing the edge of her plate with her finger. "Especially when they love and care for each other."

"Who is *your* family?" Asim asked bluntly.

"I—we only have each other." Ranya shrank in on herself. "The one other person I call family saw to that."

"Ranya's brother was planning on selling her to the Wife Market." I grabbed her hand and threaded my fingers with hers, glaring at my brother. "Instead of allowing him to do that, I have asked Ranya to marry me."

Aisha gasped. "You're getting married?" When I nodded, she squealed in excitement.

"When will this wedding be?" Father spoke at last. "I assume fairly soon?"

"Tonight," Ranya and I said in unison, and I couldn't help the smile that slipped onto my lips when she tightened her hold on my hand.

"Nicar above, everyone is lovesick." Asim snorted. "And you can't be serious! Marry *her* of all people? As the heir to the business, you should try for an advantageous match that will further—"

"Hang the business!" I snapped. "You know I don't care about an advantageous match or partnership or any of that. I care about Ranya, Asim. I know that's hard for you to understand; you always have your nose stuck in scrolls and figures and shipping schedules. But you're missing a whole world out there. A whole life." I squeezed Ranya's hand. "I found the woman I want to love for the rest of my life and I'm going to marry her *tonight* with or without your blessing."

Asim's jaw flexed, and without a word, he rose and stalked out the door.

"Well, you handled that nicely," Ravi noted.

I rubbed my neck, leaning my elbows on my crossed legs. I truly wanted Asim's approval for this, and part of me felt like I couldn't go through with it without him by my side. Ranya laid her hand against my arm, squeezing gently. Her presence brought me back to the reason for all of this, and I laid my hand over hers.

"So, a wedding tonight." Mother's eyes scanned the courtyard. "I think we can have this done up in plenty of time. Aisha, do you still have that bejeweled kaftan you wore for your engagement party?"

"Oh, yes!" She turned to Ranya, eyeing her figure like the seamstress she was. "I'm a bit bigger than you, but I think we can make it work."

"I don't want to be any trouble," Ranya protested weakly.

"Nonsense. You're going to be family." Mother squeezed Ranya's shoulders in a sort of side hug. "Family looks out for one another."

Tears flooded my betrothed's eyes as a flurry of activity began, everyone jumping to Mother's orders.

"I told you they'd love you," I said.

She leaned her head against my shoulder. "You were right."

"I'm always right." I chuckled after I kissed the top of her head. "Well, nearly always."

Ranya laughed and was quickly pulled off into the clamor of wedding preparations.

I helped move some tables, hang some gauzy curtains, and sent a servant to fetch a priest for the evening ceremony.

Father pulled me aside as the sun began its descent toward the horizon. "Are you certain about this?"

"I've never been more certain about anything." I ran a hand over my short-cropped hair. "I can't explain it, but there's a peace with this choice. I will love her until the earth fades away, Father. Nicar brought us together."

"And what Nicar has bound, let no man break," Father finished the sacred vow and clasped my shoulder. "I'll talk to Asim."

"Father." I stopped him with a hand on his arm, a thought taking root. "I have a proposition for you."

"I'm listening," he prompted when I hesitated.

"I'm not certain you'll like it."

He raised a brow, waiting.

And then I told him of my wedding present for Ranya, Asim, and most importantly, for myself.

Chapter Ten

Ranya

I had never expected my wedding day to feel so chaotically beautiful as that afternoon turned out to be. In fact, I hadn't let myself think about my wedding day much since Momma and Poppa's deaths. Somehow, I could never picture it without them at my side.

But Aisha and Qamar filled the void my lack of family presented. They dragged Nafia and Janan away from their dolls and bathed all five of us amongst bubbles, laughter, and chatter. My spirits lifted, despite the heavy weight of dread my brother had over me.

Aisha was brushing my hair in neat steady strokes when she asked, "So, what did you notice first about my brother?"

I bite my lip. "Do you want the expected answer or my honesty?"

"Honesty, always." Aisha chuckled.

"The first thing noticed about Saif was that he is an absolute flirt."

Qamar, who was busy braiding Janan's hair, tipped her head back and laughed. It was hearty and deep, not the type of laugh I expected out of the petite older woman. But her eyes sparkled when she looked at me in Aisha's vanity mirror. "You're right about that, my dear. He's been a natural born flirt since the day he was born. Between the twins, Saif was the one who was always smiling and laughing."

"Asim has always been more serious." Aisha paused. "He prefers figures to people and scrolls to conversation."

"Is he upset by…?" I gestured to me and dropped my gaze to my fingers.

"He's upset that his plan isn't a reality." Qamar sighed as she finished pinning up Janan's hair. "But the rest of the family is thrilled for you to be ours."

Janan smiled and threw her arms around Saif's mother. She choked out, "Thank you."

"Oh, my dear." Qamar looked questioningly at me, and I had to look away to keep myself from crying.

Aisha began doing my hair as Qamar did Nafia's. Once they finished, they shooed both girls back to Nafia's room.

"Now, my dear." She came over and sat across from me. I was well and truly stuck, Aisha's fingers firmly gripping my hair as she twisted it into submission. "Tell me the truth about why you're here."

"Saif asked me to marry him," I whispered, not wanting to tell this family how broken mine really was. I had found something good here in the middle city, something untainted by my harsh reality. If they knew the truth, I'd be handed pity or they'd feel a sense of duty toward me. I didn't want that. No, I longed for love and laughter and light. Something not spoiled by Majid and his drunken rage. I wanted peace and happiness. Was it too much to ask for one day of that?

"But before that?" Qamar ran her fingers down my arm, her brows worried. "I saw the bruises on your back, Ranya. Who gave them to you?"

My throat was thick as I choked out, "My brother." A shuddery breath rattled my chest, and I squeezed my eyes shut. I felt Majid's fist against my back as I shielded Gazhi. It hurt, ached down to the pit of my stomach. But I hadn't moved. Hadn't even dared to cry out. A single tear snaked down my cheek and I stubbornly brushed it away.

"Oh, my dear girl." Qamar scooted her stool closer and hugged me. "I am so sorry you had to bear that evil for not only yourself, but for your brother and sister."

"Janan said he's been that way for a long time." I sniffed. "How can a ten-year-old see what I missed?"

"Because children see the world in black and white. We see the world in glaring color. Neither is wrong. We need both to survive, I think."

"Is it bad to miss Majid? Not the way he hurt us, but the way he was before Momma and Poppa died. He used to laugh and tease. The light in his eyes has been gone for the last two years. I miss my brother." I choked back a sob, failing miserably.

Qamar pulled me away from Aisha, though I'd stopped feeling her work long ago, and simply hugged me tightly as I cried. She rubbed my back in slow circles, humming an old Talethan lullaby. Soon, my tears abated, and I focused on Qamar's steady presence. Perhaps, here with Saif's family, I'd found a place to be loved and to belong.

"I'm better now." I straightened, wiping at my damp cheeks and forcing a smile.

"Are you certain *you* want to marry Saif?" Aisha asked.

"He is the one thing in this whole mess I *am* certain about," I said with conviction. *I merely hope Saif wants me after everything is said and done.* I wasn't positive when I'd known I wanted to marry Saif, not only for protection but because I could envision our lives twined together as partners. Perhaps it was when he'd held me at the old alehouse. Or when he'd kissed me outside his home. Or the way he'd defended his choice to Asim. Whenever it had been, I was ready to marry him and bind our lives together.

Aisha glided to a wardrobe with flowers carved along the trim and pulled out a stunning red kaftan. Gold jewels were sewn along the bodice and cuffs and shimmering pearl beads marched down the back to the waist. The jewels swirled into vines, leaves, and flowers, shimmering in the light and casting rainbows along the walls and ceiling.

"I can't wear that!" I protested as Aisha hauled me to my feet.

I was already in my underthings and she began to undo the buttons on the kaftan, ignoring my protests. "I've already worn this, and besides—" her brown eyes shown conspiratorially "—I can't wait to see Saif's face when you walk up to him in this. It'll look stunning against your olive skin tone."

"I can't—"

"You can, you will, and I'll thank you to stop arguing with us." Qamar had her fists planted on her hips, one brow raised as if daring me to say another word.

Wisely, I pressed my lips into a thin line and let Aisha and Qamar transform me into a bride worthy of Saif's hand.

Yet inside, I was still terrified. Because yes—I wanted to marry Saif, wanted to jump into the new world of marriage and never look back. But I was still a woman from the lower city. What would he think of me after our vows were exchanged? He said he was here to stay, but what would keep him from changing his mind? What if he regretted his choice of wife after our wedding night? I wasn't as stunning as the women he was used to seeing. I wasn't plump with curves that caught the eye. What if he expected something from me? A beauty I didn't possess? I couldn't perform, the mere thought of what it would mean to be his *wife* petrified me. What if I wasn't...good enough?

Majid's words echoed in my ears as Qamar brushed a gold powder against my cheekbones and eyelids. *Who's going to save you? To the rest of Mordova, we're nothing but lower city gutter trash. Who would want you?*

Do you really want me? I thought as I stepped into the dress. It was cool and sleek against my skin and I couldn't help running my hand over the material. *Why would you want gutter trash? An almost street rat? You have all of this.* I looked at his smiling mother and laughing sister as tears pricked my eyes. *So why would you choose me?*

Chapter Eleven

Saif

I stared at the one room slum I stood before. My hands were curled into fists, and my breathing was slightly erratic as I stepped up to the curtain hanging slightly askew over the door.

This is a horrible idea. So why did I feel so at peace as I rapped on the doorframe?

"What do you want?" A slurred voice asked as a man—dressed in nothing but a stained pair of salwar—stumbled out of the door. His shoulder-length black hair was mussed, and his amber eyes were greatly dilated. He smelled horrible, and it took everything in me not to gag as he staggered forward.

"I'm here to tell you I'm marrying your sister." I straightened up, using my significant height difference against him.

"You're what?" Majid looked up and down the street. "Is that where the whore went? Off to you?"

I scowled. "Do not call my *intended* such a name. Yes, she came to me seeking protection from you. I asked her to marry me, as I've grown quite fond of her."

"Bed her yet?" He sneered, but his eyes went wide as I slammed him up against the doorframe.

"We're getting married. A sacred and holy thing that scum like you know nothing about." He tried to speak but I tightened my grip. "Now listen well. You will leave Ranya, Gazhi, and Janan alone. Take this money—" I threw a bag of silver in through the window "—and stay out of their lives. If I ever see you anywhere near them or my family, you're a dead man. Do you understand?"

He nodded, his face turning slightly blue. Majid gagged as I shoved a final time and stepped back.

"Majid?" A woman wrapped in nothing but a blanket leaned out the window. Her long brown hair hung around her shoulders, obscuring some of her exposed skin. "I'm bored, come back in here." Her gaze turned to me while Majid continued to gasp for breath. She studied me appraisingly, and I squirmed, supremely uncomfortable. "Or this tall drink could come quench me."

"Sorry." I grimaced and stepped back down the street. "I have a wedding to get to."

"Too bad." She cupped her chin and grinned sultrily at me. "Come back soon, handsome."

Practically running away from the house, I rubbed my prickling arms. My teeth ached from clenching them, and all I could think of was *how*? How had Ranya survived there for the last two years? The evil oozed off her brother like an infected wound. I marveled yet again at the spirit of my future bride. She was tougher than I'd given her credit for, and it hastened my steps toward home.

The house was glowing in the setting sun as I hurried in and up to my room. Father had already prepared a tub of hot water, the steam still wafting up as I stripped my dirty clothes and washed. I quickly donned my nicest pair of black salwar and a red kurta. I knew the dress Mother was planning for Ranya to wear, and this was the closest match I had. I had just finished securing the final button when a knock sounded on my door.

At my acknowledgement, Asim poked his head in. His short black hair, so like mine, gleamed wet in the lantern light and his dark brown eyes studied me as he stepped in and closed the door. He clasped his hands behind his back. "You're going to do it?"

"Yes." I met his flinty gaze. "And I know I said I'm going to do it without your blessing, but I *would* like it, Asim."

He rubbed the back of his neck—a nervous habit we both possessed—and sighed. "Father also told me of your plan."

"I already paid Ranya's brother, although I'm thinking he's too drunk at the moment. I doubt he'll remember it." I shook my head, anger causing me to grind my teeth yet again.

"But you're truly serious?" Asim came in further, his gaze a heavy weight. "You'd give me the business?"

"I never truly wanted it." I shrugged. "It's your passion."

"But it's your inheritance. It's your—"

"No. It's not." I clasped his shoulder. "Father gave me half of my inheritance to pay off Majid, and the rest will come once he passes. I gave up my place as heir to the business for you, Asim. Your love and acceptance of Ranya mean more to me than any money or title. I'm willing to get a job and work if it means I can marry the woman I love. And while I know you and the family will always be there for us, I feel like this is something I have to do. For Ranya and me, and for me and you."

Asim stared hard at me for another moment before nodding once. "Then you have my blessing. No man would go this far over mere infatuation."

I grinned. "Oh, I'm plenty infatuated with my future wife. But I also love her." *Nicar above, do I ever love her.*

Asim scoffed but smiled—the first real smile I'd seen on his face in months—and clasped me on the shoulder.

"Will you stand as my witness?" I asked, suddenly nervous. This was it. After tonight, I would be a married man with a wife to look out and provide for. I would protect her, love her, serve her. Was I ready for this?

"I will." Asim smirked knowingly. "And you'll make a wonderful husband. At least you should be better at that than business."

I chuckled, some of my nerves dissipating. "Thank you, Asim. I think."

With a final squeeze, my twin let his hand fall. "Well, I suppose it's time to get you married!"

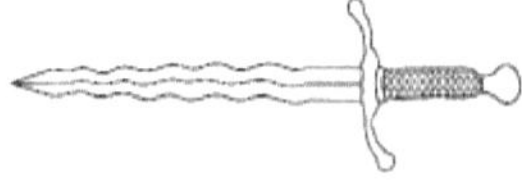

The courtyard smelled like lemon and some flower I couldn't name as I stood at the far end. I didn't know what to do with my hands and kept shifting them from clasped in front of me to behind me and back again.

"I swear if you don't hold still, I'm going to punch you." Asim hissed in my ear with a dark chuckle. I froze with my hands behind my back. It wasn't an idle threat. He'd done it before.

Aisha skipped down the steps and took her place across from me with a smile. "Here comes your bride!" she cooed.

The priest—a fat man with a thatch of white hair sticking up in all directions—waddled to the front and turned, waiting for Ranya. Mother glided down the steps and took her seat beside Father and Ravi. A few neighbors and friends were present, but on such short notice, it was mostly family. Bashar sat beside Gazhi, his arms crossed, a smile on his face as Nafia whispered in Janan's ear, both girls giggling. All four grinned at me with excitement and I returned their smiles with one of my own, as giddy about this moment as they seemed to be.

Mother cleared her throat and when I met her gaze she gestured toward the stairs. There—looking like an angel of Nicar—stood Ranya. She'd always been beautifully stunning, but in the red kaftan, with her black curls twisted into intricate braids and pinned up on her head, she was the most breathtaking vision in the world.

And she was walking toward me.

Her hands hung at her sides, and she held her head high. Her eyes fixated on me as she glided up and clasped my hands. A gauzy veil hung over her face, and my fingers itched to pull it away.

But not yet. The priest waved his incense around us, the scent of frankincense heavy in the warm air as he began the customary liturgy.

Ranya looked up at me, the vulnerability in her gaze tightening my throat. She leaned close, her eyes flicking to the priest before she whispered, "Are you certain?"

I squeezed her hands and leaned a bit closer. "Always, Ranya."

She straightened and returned to listening to the ceremony, but for me, it was all a blur. I said what I was supposed to, vowed to cherish and love Ranya. We pricked our fingers with a curved dagger then drew the proper symbols on each other's foreheads with the blood. But it was as if I were underwater. The sounds were muffled, my vision only on the woman at my side.

At long last, the priest flourished the incense stick a final time. "In the view of these witnesses, let the papers be signed, binding them in the sight of the law. Tonight, they shall be bound by flesh. What is joined this day, let no man break. Saif, you may seal your vow."

I grinned, pulling off Ranya's veil to indicate that she was mine to love, cherish, and lead until Nicar called us from the earth. Then, cupping her cheek, I leaned in and kissed her. Her arms wrapped around my neck and she swayed closer, deepening our kiss with a sigh. Applause sounded, and a wolfish whistle had Ranya pulling away and biting her lip as she grinned. I glared at Bashar who whistled again and laughed.

Ranya wrapped her arm around my waist, and I felt her tremble ever so slightly as she smiled out at our family. *Our* family. I pressed a kiss to her head as Mother and Father stepped forward, hugging us and sharing in our happiness.

Then Bashar came with Gazhi. The young boy leapt into my arms and hugged me hard. "You're my brother now?"

"Yes," I managed past the squeeze of my chest.

"You won't hit us, will you?" He pressed his hands against my cheeks, his brows furrowed.

"Never," I vowed, hugging him tightly before setting him back on his feet.

Nafia and Janan came up, arms linked. Nafia hugged me, then Ranya, before hurrying over to where the rest of the family stood around the tables of food the servants had put together.

Janan paused before me, looking up into my face with fear-filled eyes. "You'll take care of Ranya?"

"And of you and Gazhi." I knelt, uncertain I had the words to convey what I felt. "When I married your sister, I took charge of you as well. My family did. *You* are our family, Janan. My sister in all but blood. I won't leave you."

She bit her lip like Ranya. Her gaze was filled with fear and yet a hunger to be known and loved. I met her scrutiny without flinching. Finally, Janan must have found what she was searching for because she flung her arms around me, a small sob catching in her throat. "Thank you, Saif."

I rubbed her back for a minute before she leaned back and threw herself into Ranya's arms. They whispered back and forth for a moment before Ranya kissed Janan's forehead and the little girl ran after Nafia.

"Thank you for saying that to her." Ranya pulled me to my feet and wrapped her arms around my middle. "She needed to know we would be there for her."

"We will be." I rubbed Ranya's back. "Always. Family first."

She tightened her hold around me. We stood for a long moment and watched the guests laugh and talk. They all seemed genuinely happy for us, though undoubtedly the rumor mill in the middle city would explode with the gossip about our hasty wedding. But I didn't care. Ranya was my wife, my love, *mine*.

"Are you ready to go up?" I asked, suddenly very eager to be alone with my wife.

She stiffened but nodded. Something felt off as she slid her hand in mine and we hurried to say goodbye to everyone and make our way up to my room.

Aisha had laid out for Ranya a nightdress as well as a fresh kameez and salwar for the morning. When my wife's gaze fell on them, she halted so abruptly I almost slammed into her. She stood, stiff as a board, by the foot of my bed, her eyes tracking me like a desert hare, poised to run.

I raised a brow at her. "Is something wrong?"

"No, I—" Her gaze dropped. "I'm not certain what tonight will be."

"That's for us to decide." I eased closer, tipping her face up to meet mine. Caressing her cheek with my thumb, I whispered. "Whatever we want."

Her throat moved with a tight swallow and I let my lips brush against it, then up to her cheek and her lips. Ranya's hands settled on my waist, a slight moan escaping her that sent heat flooding through me. But when she shivered, I eased back.

"What do you want, Ranya?"

"I want you to promise me something." She fiddled with the buttons on my kurta. I could feel the tension in her posture as I waited for her desired vow. At last, she looked up at me. "Will you vow on Nicar?"

"Of course I will. But what am I vowing?"

"It's something I heard my poppa promise my momma one time." A dreamy look slipped across her face. "By Nicar, I promise to serve you. By the light above, I vow no secrets shall lay between us. And by love, I swear to cherish you as man ought—faithfully and forever."

I smiled, nuzzling my nose into Ranya's neck once more, and quoted the lines as she repeated them. "By Nicar, I promise to serve you." *In whatever way she sees fit.* "By the light above, I vow no secrets shall lay between us." *I want you to trust me forever, my love.* "And by love, I swear to cherish you as man ought—faithfully and forever." *Until death parts us.*

"Do you mean it?" A vulnerability lay in the tattered edges of her voice. Her chest rose and fell rapidly as I wrapped my arms around her waist. "Majid said we were street rats, gutter waste. No one should want me, Saif."

"Why do you doubt your value?" I asked, tipping her chin up. "You're beautiful, brave, fierce, protective, loving. Ranya, you radiate light. I am blessed by Nicar that you chose me, that you want me."

"I do want you. But how can you want *me*, a street rat?" Her voice caught and she shook her head.

"Because I keep my word. 'By the light, I vow no secrets shall lay between us'." I tightened my hold on her waist and let my nose brush hers. "I took care of your brother. He won't come near you again if I have any say in it. And I gave my position as heir to my father's business to Asim."

"Why would you do that?" Ranya asked.

"Because you're not comfortable here." She dropped her chin to her chest, but I tipped it up. "And you're worth far more to me than this business. I want to provide for you. Work for you. Make you as comfortable as I'm able. If it means finding a job here in the middle city to do that? I'm willing and able to work. I'm not letting you go, Rayna."

I skimmed my fingers down Ranya's neck, finding the top button of her gown and fingering it. "I'll find a job. And our family will help us."

Rayna's lips pursed and slowly she turned, giving me full access to the back of her kaftan. I leaned over her shoulder and kissed her neck again. "Are you certain?"

"Yes." Her voice shook, but it wasn't in fear. Before I could begin unbuttoning her kaftan, she turned back around and flung her arms around my neck. "Thank you for all you've done for me and my family. I—I love you, Saif."

Holding her close, I whispered. "By light and love and Nicar above, I'd do it all again and more for you, my love. All again and more."

And then I was kissing her, lost in the feel and scent and passion that was loving Ranya—my wife. The night grew long, both of us lost in the complicated dance of love. Neither of us knew the steps, but it was still beautiful because it was ours and ours alone to cherish.

CHAPTER TWELVE

Ranya

Seven years later...

"Do you have everything you need?" I asked Janan, propping my nine-month-old son on my hip as Aisha pinned a veil over my sister's black locks.

"I'm more prepared than you were when you married Saif!" Janan rolled her eyes and laughed.

I joined her and my sister-in-law in a small chuckle. Swaying my hip to keep Kadin quiet, we continued to prepare my sister to be a bride. It felt as if the last seven years had gone by in the blink of an eye. Saif was now a guard for the malek of Taletha, and we lived in a little house on the palace grounds. Kadin was a blessing we weren't certain we'd even have. Yet, Nicar had given us our son, and he was a treasure we didn't take lightly. We had loved and cared for Gazhi and Janan, but now they were old enough to forge their own ways in the world.

Gazhi had gotten a job working with Sarju and Asim as a tradesman and he was a good one. At fifteen, he was already a force to be reckoned with at the docks. I was proud of the man my brother was becoming, and thankful that both he and Janan had the guidance of Qamar and Sarju in their lives.

"Are your bags all packed?" I asked.

"Yes." Janan laughed. "And Bashar already took them to our new house." She shook her head and rolled her eyes again. "Honestly, it's like you're the one getting married, not me."

I sighed, choking back tears on the tail end of my laugh. Janan and Bashar had grown close over the years. It still amazed me that my little sister was old enough to marry—stranger still that it was to my husband's brother.

Life was odd; one minute everything was spinning out of control, hopeless, depressing, and unstable. Then a chance meeting, a smile, a greeting, and in a moment everything could change.

A rap sounded on the door and my husband poked his head in. "Everyone is ready for the bride."

Saif's eyes settled on Janan. Her white kaftan hugged her curves, the gauzy veil draped over her head and around her shoulders, while the maang teeka caught the afternoon light. Saif's mouth parted ever so slightly.

Aisha laughed, scooping up her slumbering daughter from the bed. "She's grown up a bit, brother." She bumped him with her hip and sailed out the door.

Saif hadn't moved and Janan clasped and unclasped her hands. "Do I look all right, Saif?"

"You look stunning." He shoved his fingers into his eyes and rubbed. Sighing with a shake of his head, he said, "And I can't even threaten Bashar to take care of you. Father already did a fair job of that."

Janan laughed again, her eyes welling up with tears as she embraced Saif. "Thank you for keeping your word."

"What word was that?" he asked, a hint of bewilderment in his voice.

"You promised you'd look out for Gazhi, Ranya, and me." She looked up at him, her expression full of trust and peace. "You've always been there. When that first boy broke my heart last year? You were there. When Gazhi got sick and almost died? You were there." I flinched at that horrid memory, and Saif snaked his arm around my waist, pulling me close.

"You've always been there. Thank you." Janan rose onto her tiptoes and kissed his cheek, then kissed me. "I'll be down soon. I want to say a prayer first."

"Don't keep Bashar waiting too long." Saif kissed the top of Janan's head. "I think Asim might punch him if he gets any antsier."

I laughed, Janan nodded, and then Saif guided me down the stairs. We paused on the landing and looked out over the courtyard. Family and friends we'd acquired over the last seven years chatted as the musicians played softly in the corner.

Saif sighed contentedly and pressed a kiss to my temple. "How is it possible that this is my life?"

I smiled up at him. "Because you're a good man, Saif. I thank Nicar for you every day."

"I thank her that we chose each other." He kissed my lips, then the top of Kadin's head. "And that we keep choosing one another."

"Forever, my love." I took his hand as we hurried to our seats. The chatter and laughter swelled around us and I couldn't help but smile. It had been a scary jump, taking Saif's hand that day as we stood on the old ale house roof. But as I had said that day and every day since we'd married, it was who you jumped with that mattered. And I had leapt with the very best.

Saif wrapped his arm around my shoulders as Janan walked down the steps and the ceremony started. As our siblings exchanged their vows, he leaned in and whispered against my hair, "By light, love, and Nicar above, I vow to keep choosing you, my love. Always and only you."

The End

BONUS CHAPTERS

Enjoy two bonus chapters from Anna Augustine's upcoming full-length novel, *By Blood and Blade*, set in the same world as *By Light and Love*.

CHAPTER ONE

INARA

The Wife Market of Taletha was open for business, and I was up for sale. I smoothed my trembling hands across my white satin kaftan as the short sleeves of the gown chafed against my upper arms. I stood on my block with twenty-nine other women. Straight backed, hands at our sides, eyes gazing ahead at nothing, we appeared like the beautiful marble statues of our goddess, Nicar. If only we had the power she possessed.

The large, domed ceiling kept it pleasantly cool in the large, dimly lit room. There were no windows to let in a cooling breeze or fresh air. There were only three doors: one let prospective buyers in, one allowed the men to take their brides out, and one led to our living quarters. It was the first door we all faced at the moment, although I wanted to escape out of the third door—to curl up into the blessed nothingness of sleep.

It took all my strength to remain serene and poised—*as a wife ought to be.* But inside of me raged a deep-rooted fury. No one deserved this, least of all me. I had been plucked from my home and shoved here for a couple hundred gold coins. Now we all stood, primped and pressed and molded into fake versions of perfection. We were paraded for men to gawk at and buy without even the slightest agreement from us. I was being manipulated and controlled once more.

None of this showed on my face. No, I stood with my shoulders back and head held high as another nobleman strolled by. He was dressed in the style of all young Talethans, with an embroidered vest of black covering his red kurta, flowing salwar cuffed at the ankle, and head bare of any hat. His tan skin and thick black hair displayed his heritage as perfectly Talethan—unlike my own blonde hair and blue-green eyes. The bells on the tips of his pointed shoes rang through the warehouse with every step, curling the nerves in my stomach tauter with each jingle.

He reached my block and glanced me over from the top of my head to the tips of my toes. Being first was the worst sort of punishment. It meant I had been here the longest, rejected over and over again. He stepped up on the block and stretched out his hand, fingering a strand of my blonde hair before the back of his hand caressed my jaw and then my lips. It took a staggering amount of self-control to not bite his wandering fingers, but I could see my owner, Omar, out of the corner of my eye and so I refrained.

I regretted my restraint almost instantly when the man's lip curled in an arrogant sneer. "You're a pretty thing, but it's too bad you look so *northern*." I wanted to flinch as his hand trailed down my bare arm. But seeing Omar's narrowed gaze still focused on me, I remained staring ahead, even as the noble's hands wandered to places they shouldn't. I tried to think of happy memories from my childhood, but it was nearly impossible.

Eventually, the young noble grew bored of me and moved on, slowly dismissing each girl in turn. At last, it came down to just me and Maram, one of the few girls I considered a friend. Nerves bloomed in my stomach. Like all the women, I did long to be chosen. Even a marriage against my will was preferable to Omar's harping, primping, and meddling. Any one noble would surely be better than enduring the fondling and petting of dozens of men per day, preferable to being treated like livestock. This wasn't the first time it had come down to me and one other woman, and I knew what to expect.

The young man ogled me again, his eyes practically undressing me as he stepped closer. His hands settled on my waist, and I yearned to pull away. Walling up my heart in an icy cage, I closed my eyes, not wanting to see his face.

"Look at me," he ordered, his hot breath blanketing my face and causing me to gag. I had no choice but to obey, my hands shaking at the predatory gleam of victory in his gaze. His hands roamed over me, poking and fondling once more. He took his time, enjoying my body without my leave, like I was a heifer and he a prospective buyer.

Suddenly, his hands fell away, and the look of disgust returned. He turned and walked to Maram, repeating the process with her. But unlike me, she did what was expected of her. She returned his pursuit, settling her hands on his sides, leaning in and accepting his touch, his look, his kiss. She was what he wanted. She fit the world in which we lived. With her flawless olive complexion, dark hair and eyes, she was the perfect Talethan daughter. She was exactly what the patrons of the Wife Market valued in a bride.

It was common practice in Taletha for a rich man to buy a wife—often more than one. The Market stretched across the nation, a warehouse in every major city in Taletha. I had been sold to the Market in Mordova—the city of my birth. Now, I found myself a day's journey northwest in the city of Rana.

Not that it mattered what city we were in. Kept confined to the warehouse until we were chosen, groomed, powdered, and bathed. Our sole focus, our only job, was to be bought by a man. We had to sell ourselves in whatever way necessary.

Some of the wealthier girls were trained from infancy to be the perfect wife, sold by their fathers as young as fourteen in order to secure a match. Those girls were gorgeous, the very picture of the ideal Talethan wife. They were doted on, their parents sending gifts of clothes and jewels weekly—if not daily.

In no way was I one of those girls. My father sold me and never looked back, quickly returning to the seas with my half-brothers. I hadn't heard from any of them in years and often wondered if they were even alive.

The young noble returned to my stand yet again, and I struggled to keep my breathing steady as he traced my jaw with his clammy fingers. My body shook involuntarily when he cupped the back of my neck and leaned in close. Unable to hold his gaze, I dropped my eyes, a single tear leaking from my eye.

"I choose this one." The lord proclaimed, using his free hand to point at Maram, who smiled coyly as he turned from me and extended his hand toward her, his chosen bride.

Omar clapped. "An excellent choice, my lord. Let me call our priest, and we shall deal with the necessary paperwork and ceremony. Are you planning a larger affair later?" He guided the new couple out the far door—the wedding door, as we called it—and I finally allowed myself to sag when the click echoed through the great market room.

The rest of the girls relaxed, and a small wave of conversation began as they moved toward our rooms. As my legs began to tremble, I lowered myself to the platform and buried my head in my hands.

Don't let them know that it bothers you, I ordered myself, trying to maintain the cage of ice around my heart. It had been my constant companion, my only defense, since the tender age of four when I first felt the pain of my father's fist.

Saif, my guard, knelt beside my block and offered me his hand. "I'm sorry, Inara."

"I'm fine, Saif."

The look on his face told me he didn't believe me, but he didn't press the issue. Of everyone in the warehouse, Saif was the only person I trusted. He had been assigned to me since my first day, and for six years never wavered in his devotion.

He pulled me to my feet now and tucked my hand into the crook of his elbow as he guided me back toward the wife wing. "What did you think of that man?"

It had become a game with us. What did we think of each man who spurned me on the buying block? Some were too fat, others too skinny. Some were outrageously dressed, some not dressed enough—as had been the case the day before when a palace guard had come swaggering into the Market in nothing but his under clothes. He'd promptly been escorted out.

"This one seemed like an arrogant, pompous bore."

Saif smiled, his teeth bright against his dark skin. "Yes, and Nicar knows you need someone who can admit when he's wrong."

"Yes, and he has to match my wit." I smiled up at him, thankful for the levity our conversation brought to an otherwise humiliating moment. Saif had one of the few keys to my heart, and I prayed that Omar never learned of it. If he did, he'd remove Saif as my guard, and I would die the day that happened. "Speaking of wit, how is Ranya?"

"Doing well." His eyes danced with love as he spoke of his wife. "I felt the babe kick again last night."

"Oh, how wonderful!" My smile slowly slipped as he continued on and on about Ranya, their unborn child, and their happily wedded bliss. I could never have what they did. Happiness, love, mutual respect—it was a lie I fed myself in the night. When I was lonely, I played with the *what ifs*. What if I wasn't a Market Bride? What if someone would love me for who I was as a woman and not just as a thing to be possessed? What if someone saw the raw bleeding mess that was my heart and chose to stay?

But it was only that—a lie. For I was a Market Bride, and that meant I was an object, a thing to be bartered for and sold to the highest bidder. No one would ever truly see me as a person, as a woman worthy of love and affection. The most I could hope for was a considerate man who would meet my basic needs and not force himself on me. I shivered as my imagination conjured up vivid images far too easily. The fondling I experienced on the block would be nothing to fulfilling my wifely duties, especially with a man I knew nothing about and who likely only bought me for my body. A gag choked me, and my hand rose to my throat as I struggled to think of something pleasant.

We reached the common room where the other twenty-eight women sat on cushions, munching foul and hummus on pita bread. The savory spices made my stomach churn, and I curved an arm across it.

"Oh, look girls. It's the worthless northerner." Kittim, a new arrival, sneered. "Can't seem to get a man to want you, Inara? I can give you some tips."

"Because you've been here for so long." Tirsa rolled her eyes. "I've been here a month, and I'll have you know Inara has never tried to get a man to buy her." She tossed her sleek black hair. "Have you ever returned a prospect's kiss when it's down to you and another?"

"No," I whispered, wrapping my other arm across my middle before sitting.

"No?" Kittim scoffed. "No wonder you can't get a man to choose you."

"She's too sweet," Zivah stated. Henna covered her hands, swirling and scrolling and drawing attention to her smooth, flawless skin. "She doesn't work on standing out."

Kittim giggled. "She stands out enough with that hair! Have you ever thought about dying it?"

"You can't do that!" Tirsa protested. "It's one of the laws of the Market."

"It's also against the law for the men to kiss us, but Omar allows it." Zivah shrugged her slim shoulders.

"Inara?" One of the newest girls—she couldn't have been a day over fourteen—slipped to my side, her eyes glassy.

"What is it, Talora?" I asked, weariness pressing down on me.

"I think..." she glanced down, and I noticed blood on her leg. Her monthly cycle. A sob caught in her throat, tugging on my heart as I turned toward her.

"It's all right." I cupped her cheek. "Has this happened before?"

Her head shook, tears trailing down her cheeks. "What's happening?"

My heart pinched as I remembered my own experience. My mother had been out working when my cycle first began. I thought I was dying and had curled into a ball on my bed all day with my stomach cramping terribly. It wasn't until Mother had returned the following morning and explained what was happening that I learned I would, in fact, live to see another day.

"Come on, dearest. I'll help you clean up and get ready for bed. I'll explain it all."

She sniffed, dashing away the tears with the back of her hand. "I won't be standing up tomorrow at the Market, will I?"

I knew she wouldn't. Omar didn't want anything to hinder a buyer. A man may not want us if he knew it was our time of the month.

I wrapped my arm around Talora and guided her down to our rooms. "Everything will be fine. It only lasts a few days."

Talora's room was identical to mine. Soft embroidered rugs covered the cool tiled floor while a pile of pillows and blankets served as a bed. With a small window on the far wall to let some air flow, it wasn't quite a cell, but the bars on the small opening were a constant reminder that we were indeed stuck here until some man found us worthy.

I helped Talora clean up and then tucked her into bed. Brushing her hair with my fingers, I settled into a rhythm that relaxed my shoulders and pleasantly numbed my mind.

"Have you really been here six years?" Talora asked, breaking the spell of calm.

"Yes."

Six long years of lust and leers. Six years of being almost perfect—but still lacking. Six years of seeing hundreds of others chosen and yet having rejection after rejection tossed my way. Six years of loneliness, isolation, and fear. Fear of never being good enough, never being wanted, never being loved. Once, long before the Market, there had been someone who said they loved me, but he too had rejected me. If he could so casually toss me aside, why would someone who didn't even know me ever want me?

Yet, I couldn't tell Talora that. She wouldn't understand, and I didn't want to worry her. So instead, I leaned over and pressed my lips to her forehead. "But you, my dear, are a beautiful daughter of Taletha. A man will see you and fall madly in love."

"That's a fairytale," she whispered, her eyes already half closed. "I'd be happy if he simply took care of me and fed me."

My throat felt thick, my body heavier than normal as I closed the door to Talora's room and leaned against it. I closed my eyes, trying to will the energy into my limbs to walk the fifteen doors down to my room.

"Inara?" Saif studied me, worry wrinkling his forehead. "What happened?"

"Nothing. I'm fine."

He held his arm out to me, and I was only too glad to lean on it as he escorted me to my room.

"Thank you, Saif. I will see you tomorrow."

"Inara." He didn't let go of my hand until I dragged my eyes up to meet his gaze. "If you ever need anything, let me know. You're like a sister to me, and all I want is for you to find happiness."

A tear snaked down my cheek, and I let it. I wanted to feel again, to not be so terrified of being hurt by everyone that I lived in a constant state of numbness. I let Saif in, if only a bit. But even he could be used against me. Though he was right. Even in this living hell, I wasn't alone. Inhaling sharply, I whispered, "I know."

Saif squeezed my hand before letting me slip into my room. I slumped against the door, having no desire to change my clothes and climb into my bed. Somehow, I managed to shrug out of the white kaftan and into my plain brown nightdress. Curling up on the pillows and blankets, I let the ice thaw and drip down my cheeks. I cried for Talora and her already broken view of love and marriage. For Maram—now married to a stranger who would and could do whatever he wished to her. For my mother, dead for seven years now. And I cried for myself. For the life in which I was trapped. I was a slave. A slave to the Wife Market. And I wasn't sure I'd ever be rescued from it.

Chapter Two

Dhamar

"Pardon me, Ameer Dhamar, but your father, the exalted Malek Nadar, requests your presence at the gathering of the council."

I glanced up from the parchment I'd been reading and raised my brow at my guard. "You're now my father's messenger, Zahir?"

His face didn't break from its blank expression, but laughter danced in the depths of his eyes. After twenty years of being my constant shadow, I knew Zahir almost better than I did myself.

"Did the malek say why he wanted me at the meeting?" I asked.

"No, only that he wanted you at his side right away."

With a sigh, I pushed to my feet. Whenever Father *requested* to see me, it meant he was in a foul mood and not to be trifled with. I grimaced and shoved my hands through my black curls as we stepped into the hall. I hated the council. Hated having to appear before them like I was beneath their status. They lorded their position over everyone with great pomp and arrogance despite the fact that a word from my father would relieve them of their heads.

I slid my sweaty palms against my tunic, trying to build up enough courage to enter the council chamber once we reached it. As much as Zahir was my shadow, the council chambers were the one place where guards were forbidden. I would have to enter alone.

Panic began to claw at my throat the longer we walked. I wasn't called to this room often, but when I was, it meant nothing good. The last time I'd been here, I'd been berated for my second divorce. For whatever reason, the council wanted an heir secured from me, and they were less than pleased with my ability to carry out my husbandly duties. I was blessed by Nicar that they hadn't forced the issue. If they had, it would mean an arranged marriage at best. Or royal concubines at worst.

"Will you be all right, my ameer?" Zahir asked, hand on his scimitar and eyes slanting sideways to watch me.

Helplessness swallowed my rational thoughts as I considered a council appointed match. "I can't go in there unawares, Zahir," I choked out.

"Rumors are that this council meeting is about the issues with Šeri." Zahir shrugged, turning his gaze forward once again. Most of the nobility disliked a guard at their side, preferring for them to walk either before or behind. But I liked the steady presence of my friend next to me. He'd been more of a guide to me through life than anyone else, and I valued his insight.

"What about Šeri?" I asked. "I have heard no such rumors."

"Of course not." Zahir smirked. "You're above the common gossip found in the kitchens and training yards."

I managed not to wince at the comment. Zahir meant nothing by it, but I couldn't help feeling guilty about my title and status—a discomfort that was becoming more and more familiar. I wished to do more for my people, but being ameer meant I had to obey the malek. His word was law. I could do nothing without Father's approval and that was something I rarely obtained. All I had been able to do was marry and divorce a handful of women to earn them their freedom.

Shaking away my sour thoughts, I asked, "Well, what about the gossip?"

"The towns near the border claim that they're being raided, that Šeri is stirring up trouble by stealing livestock and produce."

"But the tribesmen are herders. Why would they be stealing livestock? Nicar knows they have enough animals to tend to without stealing more." I scratched my chin, bile coating my tongue when I caught sight of the council chamber doors.

"They are only rumors, Dhamar. Gossip tends to only hold a sliver of truth—if any at all. The wise man searches for that truth before believing what he is told."

"Especially when it doesn't seem logical." I chuckled before sighing. I forced my hands to unclench as we reached the towering doors of the council chambers.

They loomed ominously over us. Carved from ebony, they were easily three times my height. Panels of a lighter wood hung on them and were etched with stories of the exploits of the people of Taletha. Battles, mostly. Bloody, death-ridden pictures of war and the lives lost to it.

I hated these doors almost as much as the room behind them, and they did nothing to calm the roiling of my stomach. I tasted blood on my tongue and only then realized I was biting it. Forcing my jaw to unclench, I took a deep breath and schooled my features into stony indifference—my mask of choice for most occasions having to do with my father and his council. Then, I stepped through the doors of death.

The space beyond was dim, smelling of dust and sweat. With no windows to let sunlight and fresh air in, it was suffocating in the narrow room. Every few feet along the roughhewn rock walls hung lanterns. They lent their meager glow to the room, illuminating the lords that sat on red cushions. I said each of their names to myself as I walked past but didn't grace their arrogance with the honor of my gaze upon them.

Lord Hakeem, Lord Mostafa, Lord Yamin, Lord Arqa, Lord Shaeen, and Lord Mulazim. They all had beards that fell to their stomachs with various shades of gray streaked in them, and their eyes glinted in the faint light as they watched me walk to the platform that held my father's throne. It was lined with blue and white tiles, the design an intricately twisted desert bloom of some kind. It was too bright and beautiful for this room shrouded with deception and filled with conniving men after their own gain.

When I am malek, this throne will replace the golden monstrosity in the throne room. I will never step foot in this room. The council can meet me in the study or—

"So, you finally decided to grace us with your presence." Father's gravelly voice barked as I knelt and fisted my hand over my heart in submission. Yet another thing I hated. This man deserved no one's respect, least of all mine.

"I came as soon as I received your message, oh my malek." I tactfully refrained from saying Zahir's name. Nicar knew my guard had taken beatings for me on more than one occasion.

"I'm sure." Father's tone was dry and had my jaw clenching. "Stand up, boy. We have news to discuss and plans to make."

Boy. Twenty-five years, and yet I was still *boy.* My teeth ached as I stood and moved to the side of the throne, hands clasped behind my back. It had been this way for years—me silently enduring his belittling to protect the people who mattered to me. I couldn't stop the malek, but I could try to contain him.

"Now to business. We have to decide what to do about these Šerian scum. They cannot be allowed to plunder our borders without consequences. I won't hear of it!" Father banged his meaty fist against the arm of his seat, spittle flying from his lips in his rage.

Lord Shaeen steepled his fingers, tapping each one in turn as he spoke. "Do we know these rumors to be true?" He looked over at my father, his black eyes shining like onyxes in the light of the lantern by his head. His voice was raspy, reminding me of the hiss of an angry cobra.

"We do," Lord Hakeen boomed, shaking his meaty fist in the air. His jowls quivered as he shouted, "I warned of this, did I not? They've been too free in crossing between our land and their own. We should have hammered them into the sand of their godforsaken wilderness long ago!"

"Come now, Hakeen. Calm yourself. They are far more lucrative than we often credit them." Lord Mostafa said. His arms were crossed, and he leaned against the stones with closed eyes. "Surely you haven't forgotten that our rania blessed us with Ameer Dhamar. She bore a son when none of the malek's other wives were fruitful."

I struggled not to gag. My family didn't have great fortune with marriages, and my father was by far the worst. While he had remained married to my mother and claimed her to be the rania of Taletha, he still had his previous wives as well as a number of concubines in the harem. It made me ill. He kept my mother confined in her room, only calling her out when his flesh was hungry. My mother never complained, never uttered a word of anger or sadness, but I could tell she was unhappy. It wasn't how I wanted to live my life. If I ever married for a fifth and final time, I wanted it to be for love, to have a partner to live through the highs and lows with.

"Enough about my wife." Father batted away the comments as if they were a fly. "There are more pressing issues. What are we going to do about Šeri?"

"Have they attacked our people?" I dared to ask, drawing the gazes of all seven men.

"No." Lord Arqa—the head of our military—finally muttered, his gray eyes dull, and his overly-puffy lips turned down in a frown. "Unfortunately."

"Then I suggest we wait. We cannot attack until provoked." I cut a glance at my father and inwardly winced at the ice-cold glare. The stuffy room choked me, and I fell silent, fixating on the bead of sweat sliding between my shoulder blades.

"Lord Arqa, what is the state of our soldiers?" Father barked.

The man shrugged. "General Beeran's last report stated that there are fifteen hundred men able to fight within Mordova—or thereabouts—with another two thousand in Rana and Nasaria. In the smaller towns, there are around five hundred men each."

"It will take time to call up the men from all the towns, even Mordova." I spoke up again, ignoring the growl emanating from my father. "I counsel caution, oh my malek, until we know the numbers of the tribesmen."

"They are nomads, worthless." He spat to the side and growled again. "But I do agree in part. Before we go to war, there is one small matter we must see to."

All eyes swiveled to me, and I unconsciously took a step back, blood going cold.

I was right. Nothing good ever comes from this room. Nothing at all.

"The matter we must see to, as your father has stated, is the issue of your marital status, Dhamar." Lord Shaeen—the vilest of all the lords—smiled, and my mouth went dry. It was rumored that he had over twenty women he frequently bedded, but as Zahir had reminded me, it was only a rumor. Yet the predatory gleam in his brown eyes lent some credence to them.

"Yes, is it true you've divorced yet another woman?" Lord Mulazim scoffed. "Why not start your own harem? You've been married four times now."

"And all from the Wife Market, if I'm not mistaken." Lord Mostafa raised a brow, no judgment in his gaze. Of all the lords here, he was the wisest. Level-headed and fair. Perhaps the only one who would understand.

"Yes." I clasped my hands behind my back and met each of the six gazes, ignoring my father at my side. "I don't wish to have a harem. I only wish for the right woman."

"Well, you have one final chance to pick the *right* woman." Father spat again. His gray mustache quivered as he frowned, the flickering light making the oils on his black beard gleam. Sweat beaded on his olive skin. "Or I will pick one for you."

"What?" I glance at him in disbelief.

"We need an heir!" Hakeem smacked his fist into his palm. "We cannot wait much longer, especially if war is on the horizon. You will be going into war, Ameer Dhamar, like it or not. If you were to die, where would that leave us?"

I'm sure I have plenty of half-sisters hidden away. Surely one of them has a son by now. I bit my tongue and focused on the sweat on my back once more. Anything to escape this horrible conversation.

"What do you suggest?" I manage to choke out, feeling blackness edging my vision.

"One last chance at the Markets." Shaeen began tapping his fingers again. "Only this time, it will be a spectacle. You shall visit Rana's Markets as well as ours. You will observe many women until you settle on one."

"You will marry her there." Mostafa smiled, and it was almost kind. "And then a litter will bring you both back where the formal, three-day ceremony will be performed."

"It will be a holiday for Mordova." Arqa huffed. "A waste of a workday."

No one paid him any mind as they began to talk among one another, ignoring Father and me. My father grasped my arm tightly, sending tingles up into my shoulder from the pressure. "You will consummate this marriage, boy."

"What?" Surely, I heard wrong. Heat that had nothing to do with the temperature of the room flooded through me.

"I know the truth of those other marriages. You will marry this one in all ways, and you will produce an heir. If the woman you marry fails to give you a son quickly enough, you will find someone who can."

Disgust curled my lips at the implication, and I wasn't quick enough to hide it. Father stood, looming over me, his brown eyes as cold as the ice that we brought in from the east. The conversations hushed, all eyes on us.

"This is not open for discussion, Dhamar. This is a command not only from your father, but your malek."

And the malek's word is law. I squeezed my eyes shut, balling my hands at my side. Rage bubbled in my chest, but I didn't let it crack my indifferent veneer. "May I go?" I asked.

"Yes." Father stepped back, smoothing his hands over his ample stomach. He flicked his fingers toward the door dismissively. It took every ounce of my self-control to walk, instead of run, down the aisle.

"Oh, and Dhamar?"

I paused, hand on the knob and turned toward my father once again. His face was shrouded in shadows that almost seemed to dance over him in his black kurta and salwar.

"Remember. If you fail to do what I say, your mother will suffer the consequences."

My blood turned to ice. I nodded and stepped through the ebony doors. They grated closed behind me with a thud of finality. I leaned against the tiled wall, burying my face in my hands.

Zahir gripped my shoulder. "Ameer? What happened?"

"War," I choked out.

Zahir swore. When I still didn't move, he asked, "And?"

"And a wife from the Market." I looked up, fear etching its way across my heart. "A real marriage this time. I can't do that, Zahir. I don't know how."

"Well, you better start learning and soon." Zahir stood, hand settling on his scimitar as he scanned the hall. His gaze cut back to me. "Because it looks like you're going to be a husband, like it or not."

Acknowledgments

Thank you to my family, for putting up with all my scribblings and ravings about fictional characts. I couldn't do any of this without your supports.

Thank you to Quill & Flame Publishers for believing in my stories and pushing them to be the best they can be!

Thank you to my online support system for cheering me on! Thank you for spreading the word about my books and pushing them into the hands of unsuspecting readers. *cue evil laugh*

Thank you to my readers for making this writer an author! You're amazing and I appreciate each and every one of you!

Last but most importantly, thank You, Jesus. Thank you for the gift of storytelling, for blessing me with imagination and creativity so that I can dimly reflect how very creative You are!

THE AUTHOR

Anna Augustine has always loved telling stories that speak truth and hope into the lives of her readers. The author of two novella collections, *When You Found Me*, and *A Love Like Ours*. She has been published multiple times with Havok Publishing and has been in multiple anthologies including *Fool's Honor* and *Aphotic Love*. Anna is excited to be part of Q&F Publishing.

IF YOU WANT TO READ MORE BOOKS LIKE

QUILL & FLAME PUBLISHING HOUSE
HAS YOU COVERED

HEAT WITHOUT THE SCORCH

Quill & Flame
PUBLISHING HOUSE

www.quillandflame.com